Bad

VLG - Book Ten

Vampires, Lycans, Gargoyles

By Laurann Dohner

Redson by Laurann Dohner

Rescued as a child by her grandpa, the powerful Vampire Malachi, Emma has been on the run for nearly forty years from a Vamp determined to see them both dead. When he enlists the aid of assassins from the Vampire Council, their luck runs out. Forced to separate, Malachi sends Emma to a trusted VampLycan for protection.

Redson knows trouble when he sees it, and sure enough, the gorgeous, mostly human female seeking shelter immediately disrupts his future plans. His father swore a blood oath to her grandfather, and Red is honor bound to protect her. He's surprised when his instincts demand so much more—protect…claim…mate.

Their attraction is explosive, but Emma refuses to consider mating while her grandfather is in danger. She needs Red's help…but is he Malachi's savior? Or his biggest threat yet?

VLG Series List

Drantos

Kraven

Lorn

Veso

Lavos

Wen

Aveoth

Creed

Glacier

Redson

Redson by Laurann Dohner

Copyright © June 2018

Editor: Kelli Collins

Cover Art: Dar Albert

ISBN: 978-1-944526-91-7

ALL RIGHTS RESERVED. The unauthorized reproduction or distribution of this copyrighted work is illegal, except for the case of brief quotations in reviews and articles.

Criminal copyright infringement is investigated by the FBI and is punishable by up to 5 years in federal prison and a fine of $250,000.

All characters and events in this book are fictitious. Any resemblance to actual persons living or dead is coincidental.

Prologue	6
Chapter One	11
Chapter Two	28
Chapter Three	47
Chapter Four	64
Chapter Five	90
Chapter Six	108
Chapter Seven	126
Chapter Eight	145
Chapter Nine	160
Chapter Ten	173
Chapter Eleven	190
Chapter Twelve	203
Chapter Thirteen	218
Chapter Fourteen	231
Chapter Fifteen	247

Redson – VLG – Book Ten

By Laurann Dohner

Prologue

Thirty-six years in the past

Emma stared in horror at her neighborhood. Someone had dragged a recliner into the street and set it ablaze. A home down the street also had fire shooting out of the top-floor windows. A faint scream sounded from nearby. Her mother cursed softly.

Two men seemed to appear out of nowhere. They had pale skin and wore all black clothing with matching caps. Both reminded Emma of robbers she'd seen in movies on television, minus the masked faces.

Her mother jumped between her and the men.

"Why are you doing this? You're not allowed to attack us!" Her mother's voice rose in anger and she reached back, yanking out the long blade that she'd shoved into the waistband of her skirt belt. "We're under the protection of Master Malachi. Stop this, Eduardo."

One of the scary men stepped forward. Emma saw his sharp fangs and the blood that covered his cheeks and lower mouth. "We don't take orders from him anymore. He's grown soft."

"This is wrong!" Emma's mother shouted. "Leave these people alone. Are you trying to bring attention to our kind? You can't attack humans without facing consequences. You're killing them!"

"Our kind? You're *nothing* like me. These humans are harboring some of you half-breed bastards. They deserve death!" He spat blood on the ground but then a cold smile curved his lips. "You offend me, Kallie. I can imagine why Malachi wants to keep you around, but you're an abomination I refuse to abide anymore."

"You think he won't kill you for this?"

"He made me. I'm the chosen one!" Eduardo snarled. "You're a birthed mistake. Is that *your* child lurking behind you?"

Emma's mother shook her head. "I only babysit her. Stop slaughtering my neighbors. They don't even know what we are."

"You should be aware of history." Eduardo withdrew a sword. "Life isn't fair, and people die all the time after making the wrong associations. They deserve to be wiped out. I'm going to remove your head and then suck that child dry."

A roar tore through the night—and another scary man advanced. This one wasn't dressed like the others and didn't wear anything to hide his head. He had long white hair, wore jeans and a gray sweater, and he held two long swords in one of his hands. Emma had seen him before. He sometimes showed up late at night after she was supposed to be asleep. Her mother let him inside their home and they'd talk in whispers.

"Eduardo!" His deep, rumbling voice sounded terrifying. "I forbid you to attack them. Cease this nonsense immediately!"

The one threatening her mother spun to face him. "I don't listen to you any longer. And I don't trust them being so close to our nest, Malachi. I don't care *who* she is to you. They could kill us while we sleep!"

The white-haired man moved fast, grabbing the other man by the throat and throwing him. The body sailed a good fifteen feet until it slammed into a tree. He then attacked the second man. He fisted a blade in each hand, running one long sword through him. The second sword removed his head. It hit the ground and rolled. The body turned into white ash, blowing away in the light wind.

Emma whimpered.

"Run," the white-haired creature hissed softly, glancing at her mother. "I can't hold them all back. He brought in another nest. Take the child and I'll keep them off you."

"Can't you stop this?" Her mother lowered her weapon.

"There are too many. Mine are refusing to take orders from me. Eduardo has made them paranoid that you'll turn on us. I sense at least two dozen unknown Vampires coming from the other nest. Those idiots started a fire on the roads leading in here. Your only way out is through the woods. Run, Kallie. Take the child and go." Agony twisted his features. "I'm sorry. I thought this could work. I never should have put the nest together. I believed you'd be safer with our protection. Instead, it's put you both in danger."

"I'm the one they're after." Her mother glanced back, tears streaming down her face. "I love you, Emma. Remember that, baby. You do whatever this man tells you. Always trust him. He's not evil, and he'll do anything to protect you."

"Kallie," the man took a step closer but her mother darted away.

"I'll distract them and lead them away. You're fast enough to outrun them. Get her to safety. She's what really matters. I love you." Her mother ran down the street toward a group of men who stepped into sight. "Here I am!"

"No," the white-haired man hissed. "No!"

More of the black-clad men rushed from the other side of the block to surround her mother. The blond man spun, storming toward Emma. He dropped his weapons and lifted her from the ground. "Hold on, my sweet. Bury your face against my chest."

Tears blinded Emma. The blond stranger secured her tighter in his arms and sprinted as if their lives depended on it. She glanced to the side once but he moved so fast it made her feel sick.

The screams faded, the darkness complete. Sometimes she felt him jump, a sense of falling, before he'd land. His arms cushioned her from the worst of it.

It seemed forever before he stopped. He bent, setting her on her feet. He then sat, pulling her onto his lap. The sounds of his soft sobs and his chest heaving told her he cried. He rubbed her back.

"It's nearing dawn and we're inside a cave. They won't find us. You're safe, Emma."

"Where's my mommy?"

He sniffed. "She loves you very much. Do you want to know a secret?"

She wasn't sure, sensing he was something to fear. Her mommy had warned her about pale-skinned men who might appear in the night. They were the things that could take people away forever. It confused her that her mommy wanted her to trust one of them.

"I'm your grandfather, little one. Your mom was..." He sniffed loudly again. "*Is* my daughter. She might have made it past them. She was always a good fighter. I trained her. She'll meet up with us later if she's able. She knows where I'll take you. We're going to travel as soon as the sun goes down, to somewhere safer. Nothing is ever going to happen to you. Never trust a night crawler."

Fear edged up her spine. She was tired, hungry, and scared. "You're one of them."

He rubbed her back again and hugged her closer to his big body. "I'm your grandpa though. I'm the exception. I'd die for you."

"I want my mommy."

"I know, baby." He sniffed again. "I want my daughter too. She's fast though. She's a good fighter, and we have to have faith that she was able to get away."

Emma huddled against him to keep warm and finally slept. She dreamed about her mommy but then the bad men came. She woke to strong arms tightening around her.

"Shush, little one. I'm here. I'll always be here." Her grandfather, the night crawler, crooned in the darkness.

Chapter One

The present

"Emma!"

She nearly fell off the ladder from being startled. The dusting rag did hit the floor, her plans to clean the shelves forgotten. "Damn it, Grandpa!" She turned her head but he wasn't in the room. She closed her eyes, cleared her mind, and concentrated her thoughts. *"You shouted?"*

"Our enemies are close. I feel them."

Fear gripped her. *"No."*

"Yes. Modern technology is a nightmare. They are coming."

She opened her eyes and climbed down the ladder, fleeing the library. *"Where are you?"*

"In my room. Grab your bag."

"How close are they?"

"Too close. I was distracted and didn't notice them at first."

She cut the mental connection, charging up the stairs. Her bedroom was the first door on the left. She dropped to her knees, plunging her arm under the bed until her hand hit her emergency go bag. A groan tore from her as she dragged the heavy thing out and stood, shouldering the strap. The side zipper was already open and she clutched the handgun.

"Grandpa?" She used her voice this time, too frazzled to try to reach him through their family bond as she left her room. "I'm ready."

Her grandfather stormed out of his bedroom, looking anything but elderly with his shoulder-length white hair, near perfect completion, clear blue eyes, and sporting a tank top and tight jeans. Her friends always hit on him, thinking they were siblings. It never ceased to gross her out.

She did have to admit he was an attractive man for being well over four hundred years old. He would forever appear to be in his mid to late twenties in human years, since he was a Vampire.

"Where's your bag?" She frowned.

"I sensed them too late. They're already outside. You need to go. I'll stay until it's safe for me to sneak away."

"No! We stay together."

The doorbell rang, as if on cue. Emma nearly pulled the trigger just out of terror.

"Easy." He gripped her shoulders. "Hide your bag inside the escape passage, and you know what we have to do. You'll be my blood slave until I send you out of the room. We've talked about this."

"I can't!" Panic struck.

"They have us surrounded." He cocked his head. "Four are at the door, six more are approaching the house. I sense them on our hill. They are too near the exit for us to make it. But they are young. We can pull this off. They'll smell you and keep searching the house until you're found. You need to hide in plain sight."

"I suck at acting!"

"You do not. I've trained you well. You've got this."

That was easy for him to say. He always seemed fearless. He took her bag from her shoulder.

"But—"

"It's too late. They are here—we're trapped. I'll hide the bag. Wait until dawn to flee and I'll follow you as soon as it's safe. Don't make me take over your mind. It sickened you the last time."

The memory of the killer headache and a day of vomiting calmed her a lot. "I can do it."

He chuckled. "That's my girl."

The doorbell rang again and someone beat on it three times.

She stepped closer and tilted her head to the side. "Do it."

A grimace marred his features. "I'm sorry."

"This is an emergency. That's the rule. We have to make it look good."

"Damn." His fangs elongated.

Emma forced her muscles to relax and sealed her lips tight. It would only make his guilt worse if she made a pained noise. The other alternative was for him to lick her neck until the saliva from his tongue numbed the area. She didn't want either of them to suffer that indignity.

Her grandfather's fangs hurt as he bit into her. He only created a wound, didn't drink, and pulled back immediately. He refused to meet her gaze as he licked his thumb, running it over the spot to stop the bleeding.

"They'll see that. I'll put your bag away. Get the door before they break it in."

The injury burned a little but it would take less than an hour for the wound to completely heal. She rushed down the stairs and pushed her hair back to make the bite visible. She paused by the door. One glance upward at the landing assured her that her grandfather had moved out of sight. She slowly counted to four before taking a deep breath.

"Who is it?"

"Open the door!" The female voice surprised her.

"I'm not allowed to do that." She took a few steps away from the door and moved to the left.

In seconds, someone kicked the door hard enough to break the locks and three Vampires shoved their way inside. They entered the house as if they owned the place.

Emma swallowed down her fear at seeing the deadly trio. The woman was tall and had taken the Gothic-punk look to heart. Her two male companions resembled middle-aged thugs with a thing for holes in their jeans and outdated band T-shirts.

The woman glared at Emma and pointedly stared at her throat. A frowned twisted her lips downward. The fourth one her grandfather had sensed probably hid outside, prepared to pounce if they needed help.

"Where is your master?"

"I'll never tell!" Emma backed up more.

The woman advanced—but her grandfather cleared his throat loudly from above, halting the enraged Vamp set on changing her mind with pain and agony. It was his way of making a grand entrance.

"You dare invade my home? Who the hell are you? Get away from my blood slave."

Emma glanced at her grandfather as he gripped the banister, storming down the curved staircase looking every inch the terrifying creature he could be. His fangs were extended, his features harsh with rage, and his voice had dropped to that scary, "you're in deep shit and I'm pissed" tone he'd never used on *her*, even when she'd done something seriously wrong.

The sensation of menace radiated from him and even Emma couldn't ignore it. Chills ran down her spine. Her grandfather exerting his age and strength wasn't a pleasant experience to be around for a human. It did even worse things to Vampires, judging by the way the three intruders backed up with fearful expressions.

The woman seemed to be in charge, and she dropped to her knees first. Her head bowed, and the two thugs quickly followed her lead.

"I'm sorry," the woman whispered. "We meant no disrespect."

"Bullshit," her grandfather thundered. "You entered my home without permission and threatened my slave."

The woman glanced up. "I'm Paula. I serve the Vampire Council." She paused. "You aren't known to them, and we were sent to investigate."

"When did it become law to join?" Her grandfather thundered. "I'm probably older than every member. Next, they'll want me to support them. My money is my own."

Paula shook her head and kept low to the ground. "No. We're looking for rogues."

"Do I look like one of those heathens? Do you think I broke into this home and killed the owners?" He snorted. "I'm not a savage who puts our kind at risk by breaking human laws or making them investigate murders. *Leave.*"

She didn't budge. "We ask for lodging. We're far from a known nest and seek day shelter."

Emma didn't dare glance at her grandfather again. She kept her gaze on the floor but could see everyone from the corner of her eye. A real blood slave wouldn't feel much curiosity. Their wills would have been too broken to care about anything going on around them except their master's demands.

"Fine. I don't want you to have to take refuge with my neighbors. They have those security cameras that are linked to the internet where protection companies can view them. The risk of you being caught are too high. But I'm not allowing you to fuck up my peace. You may stay the day but then you will leave."

Emma realized her grandfather was trying to protect the people who lived in the homes nearest them by implying he knew them well enough to be familiar with their security measures. It would keep the Vampires from trying to feed off them. The threat of Vampires being filmed in action would assure the humans' safety. The council would ash any Vampire who made the news by being stupid and exposing the world to their existence.

"More of us are outside."

"I'm aware." Her grandfather crossed his arms over his chest. "I sensed you coming for miles. You should really work on your stealth abilities if you're rogue hunters. If I *were* one, I'd have fled long before you made it to the door." He paused. "You may hunt your meal in my woods but avoid other properties. Their cameras really are everywhere. I live here year-round."

"Hunt? As in animals? You don't have bagged blood?" The woman sounded irritated.

"No, I do not. I keep under the radar of humans. Buying blood would draw too much attention. I'm also over four hundred years old. Bagged blood is for you modern children."

The woman and two men lifted from the floor. Paula turned her head to peer at Emma. A low growl came from one of them.

It gave her the willies to be studied that way but she refused to look up. She knew how a rat must feel, cornered by three hungry cats. She concentrated on her breathing and heart rate to stifle her fear.

"Not her. She's *mine*," Her grandfather announced in a cold tone. "She's a rare type I just acquired, and I don't share."

Paula turned away. "Where are your other slaves?"

"Dead. I haven't replaced them yet. She supplies all my needs. You will find some large animals nearby." He snorted. "Be happy I'm offering that. Next time, send a letter of intent to lodge here if you expect warm meals at your disposal. Perhaps you've spent too much time hunting rogues and have forgotten proper manners."

Paula tried to protest but her grandfather cut her off. "Slave, go to my room now. Undress and get into my bed. I have other needs besides your blood."

Emma fled, ignoring the "ewww" factor of his implied intent. He wanted her away from the Vamps—now. She quickly walked out of sight upstairs but paused around the corner to listen.

"We need human blood," Paula protested.

"You should have brought your own then. I killed the four slaves I had. They were too weakened and frail to use anymore. One of them nearly burned down my kitchen."

Emma winced at the reminder. *She'd* been the one who'd done that…but the damage hadn't been too bad. She'd been baking and used too much yeast in her cake mix. The batter had spilled over into the oven, catching fire. She had managed to clean most of the smoke stains from the walls and ceiling.

"You could share the girl." It was one of the male Vamps who spoke.

"I could but I won't. She's my only source at the moment. I haven't tired of her enough to allow you to bleed her to death. I wouldn't lend you my *clothes*, so I certainly wouldn't allow you to share my slave." His voice deepened. "Who else approaches?"

Paula hesitated. "No one."

"You lie," her grandfather accused.

"*Emma?*" His voice filled her head. "*Get to the roof. It's a trap. Eduardo coming. He's with them. This changes everything. Avoid our safe house. Last resort.*"

Terror gripped her as the memory surfaced from her childhood. Eduardo was the monster who had taken her mother away, attacked the small town where she'd lived, and changed her life forever. It also meant that she wasn't going to hide in the same state. She'd have to take off on her own—and Grandpa wouldn't be joining her right away.

"Emma! Answer me. Grab your bag and get on the damn roof. You know what to do. The sun will rise soon and they're young enough to need shelter before dawn breaks. They won't have time to chase you down the mountain."

She forced the fear back and concentrated. *"I don't want to go without you! We should leave together. I'm not abandoning you to face that asshole alone."*

"It's too late. Six more of them entered the house and two of them are eyeing the stairs. Go. I love you."

"He'll kill you!"

"He could try but he'd fail. I'm his master. You're a weakness to me if it comes down to a battle. He also knows he'd break our laws by attempting to kill me in front of Vampires not under his control. The council frowns upon youths killing the ones who made them. They fear the same fate will befall them. These children aren't ones Eduardo made. They smell different. Move your ass and remember what I always told you. Reach safety and remind my old friend that it's a blood oath he swore. Tell him the truth about who you are and the entire situation. Go! They're inching closer to the stairs."

"I love you. You better come for me soon."

"It's a promise. You look just like your mother. Eduardo can't see you. He'd kill you just to hurt me. Hurry! Love you too, my little one."

Emma opened her eyes and crept down the hallway to the wall. She pushed on two spots with her index finger and thumb, then passed through the doorway that silently opened. The door closed behind her. Automatic lights came on and she hoisted her bag, laying on the floor where her grandfather had placed it. Instead of moving to the ladder that ran to the basement, she took the one up to the roof. Fear made her cautious but it also urged her to hurry.

"Tell me when you're ready. I'm going to distract them." Her grandfather's voice in her head had a soothing effect on her panic.

She climbed faster, scared of what might happen to him if he fought all those Vamps by himself. It tempted her to turn around but he was right. She'd only be a weakness. They were too fast and strong for her to fight. They'd capture her, and her grandfather would be at their mercy to keep her alive. It sucked but it was also reality.

She reached the top, unlocked the bolt to the access hatch, and pushed. The section above her opened and she climbed out onto the roof. Two large chimneys hid her from the ground. She closed the hatch, turned, and put on her backpack.

The moon shone from above, making it a clear night. It was a blessing and a curse. She could see better but so could anyone on the ground, once she left the safety of the chimneys. City lights of the town nestled in the valley far below beckoned. Their home sat in the woods, high on a hill, and the view had always been spectacular. Tonight, it sent her into a near panic attack.

"Are you ready?"

She closed her eyes, pushing her thoughts at her grandpa. *"Give me two minutes and I'm out of here."*

"Be careful."

"I hate this, by the way."

"I know."

"I'd have real wings if I were meant to fly. Are you sure you're going to be okay?"

"I swear. They wouldn't dare kill me. I'm too strong. I need you gone, honey. You're a distraction."

"I know. Promise me that you'll be okay?"

"I do. Get a move on. Two minutes and counting. Ignore the noises you hear. Eduardo is speaking to someone in the front yard and about to enter the house. Safe landing."

She grabbed the device hooked to the chimney on her right and softly cursed as she ripped off the protective plastic. Once it was freed, she opened the horrible contraption. The wind instantly tried to tear it from her fingers but she managed to clip on the straps and step into the harness. They'd practiced it a thousand times.

"Fly, angel. I love you. He's here."

She picked up more than his thoughts. She felt his fear through the link…and she paused. *"Grandpa?"*

He didn't answer.

"Grandpa?"

Still no answer. Faint shouts sounded from below. Terror made her stumble forward. The wind caught the wide wings of the glider and it propelled her forward. She staggered along to prevent herself from being dragged.

Then her feet skidded off the edge of the roof.

She dropped and swung crazily, but the wind caught the glider. It jerked her along. She sailed over trees on the way down the mountain. Fear motivated her to steer, aiming toward the city lights.

* * * * *

"Miss?"

A hand jerked Emma awake from her nightmare and she stared at the bus driver with wide eyes.

"We're here."

Not a nightmare, she thought, sitting up from where she'd slumped on the seat against her bag. She met the man's gaze with a forced smile.

"Thank you."

He turned away, moving toward the front. She gripped her bag and peered out the dirty windows of the bus. The place looked small. It appeared more of a tourist trap than a real town. She sighed, dreading whatever she'd face.

"Great. Up note, how hard can it be to find this guy in a town this small?"

No one answered, since she was alone on the bus. A bad sign that nobody wanted to visit such a remote area. The bus only came there because she'd paid hundreds of dollars for the driver to go off the normal route. The tiny town wasn't on the normal schedule. Some begging, pleading, and a sob story—and lots of money—had done the trick though.

She made her way off the bus with her bag slung on her shoulder. The driver talked to the gas station attendant while she headed for the only gift shop in town. It seemed the logical place to go, since the gas station might be part of a chain. She needed to find a resident.

A tall, beautiful, black-haired woman stood behind the counter, cleaning the glass countertop near the register. The shop didn't have any other customers. Emma approached with a yawn. She'd had to take three flights, a train, and had spent over nineteen hours total on half a dozen bus rides to reach the town named Howl. Hunger and exhaustion had taken its toll.

"May I help you?" The woman peered at her with dark, intense eyes.

"I hope so." She took a deep breath. "I'm looking for a man named Redwolf."

The woman tensed and the fingers holding the cloth tightened. "Who?"

"Klackan Redwolf. Do you know him?"

"Who are you?" The woman's voice seemed to deepen.

A tinge of alarm shot through Emma, and she took a step back. Danger radiated from the other woman. Emma could feel it as though it were a blast of frigid air. Every instinct told her to flee. She held her ground instead.

She swallowed hard. "I'm the granddaughter of a friend of his. I was sent here."

The woman's eyes turned black and the whites of them mostly disappeared.

Emma knew without a doubt she'd found one of the town's true residents.

"Who is your grandfather?"

"I'm only supposed to talk to Mr. Redwolf." She backed up another step and darted a glance around the shop to make sure they were still alone. She met the other woman's terrifying gaze. "Klackan Redwolf and my grandfather really *are* friends. He sent me here to relay a message. It's not threatening or anything."

"Talk," the other woman snarled.

"I'm in danger, and Mr. Redwolf owes my grandfather a favor," she blurted. "He sent me here to be protected."

The woman rounded the counter, her movements way too swift and fluid to be mistaken for those of a human. "From who? What kind of danger follows you?"

Emma bumped into a rack of dresses and froze. "Vampires. They didn't follow me but they found my grandfather."

"Fuck!" The woman spun away. She grabbed the phone but kept her attention on Emma as she blindly punched in numbers. "Don't move. Are you sure they didn't follow you? Who knows you came here?"

"Just my grandfather. I was very careful."

"Your kind are stupid. You make mistakes."

"It was my grandpa's plan. He's the smartest person I know."

"*All* of you are stupid." She spoke into the phone. "A human woman is in my shop looking for Klackan. She claims her grandfather was a friend of his and she's been sent here for protection from him." She paused. "Vampires." She hung up and glared at Emma. "Those bloodsuckers will be coming for you if you rate a high enough threat to them. What did you do?"

"Nothing. I don't deserve to be hunted. They won't be able to track me here. I was careful and followed my grandpa's plan to the letter."

"Humans don't know the minds of those bastards."

She hesitated. "He does."

"Bullshit! What makes him an expert?"

Emma didn't want to answer. The woman really seemed to hate Vampires.

"That's what I thought. Stupid humans think they know about us. This is why it's forbidden to tell your kind about others."

They had a stare down that Emma lost. The woman scared her. A low growl came from the woman. Maybe the truth was needed.

"My grandfather is a Vampire," she admitted. "He's been hiding me from them since I was a young girl."

Shock widened the other woman's eyes. "That's impossible. Vampires don't breed."

"We both know that's not entirely true. You're proof of that, aren't you? So am I."

Surprise stamped the woman's features. "Just stand there and wait." The woman glared at her as time seemed to crawl by.

The door finally opened to the shop and a tall, scary man stormed inside. The sight of the towering, muscled mass of masculinity with shaggy light brown hair made Emma gasp. He had huge arms, as if he lifted weights all day, and a chest so thick he could have been a breathing tree trunk. His dark brown gaze fixed on her when he came to a halt. She also noticed his facial hair. It wasn't something she usually liked but it looked sexy on him.

"Klackan Redwolf?" Hope sounded in Emma's shaky voice.

His full lips twisted downward at the corners to reveal his unhappiness. A soft growl rumbled from him next. "I'm his son. My father is dead. Start talking fast. Who are you? Why are you here? What do you want with my father?"

"Oh no! That can't be!" Despair hit, followed closely by dread. She realized her response had probably been a bit rude. "I'm...I'm sorry for your loss."

The man snarled again and took a threatening step forward. "Who are you and what do you want?"

She wanted to flee, maybe cry, or perhaps do both at the same time. "I'm Emma." She hesitated. "My grandfather is Malachi. He's technically known as Master Malachi. He's a Vampire," she added, in case that wasn't enough to clue him in. "Your father owed him a blood oath and I came to collect. I needed his protection."

His harsh features slightly softened, the darkness of his eyes lightened, and his mouth relaxed. He glanced at the woman. "It's okay, Peva. I've got this."

"Should I call a meeting? Maybe have someone dig a hole to bury her in?"

Emma's entire body quaked but she tried to hide it. She really hoped they didn't plan to kill her. She wanted to protest but kept her lips sealed.

Nothing she could say would save her life if they decided to take her out. She might as well just bend over and kiss her ass goodbye.

He ran his fingers through his shoulder-length mane of hair. "Stop joking around to amuse yourself by terrorizing a human, Peva. It's my duty to protect her."

"You know what she's talking about?"

"Yes." The guy didn't sound thrilled as he focused on Emma again. "Her grandfather has a history with my father. They really were friends. His debts are now mine, which means the blood oath has been called in." He narrowed his gaze and studied Emma slowly from head to toe. "Great. Just what I needed. Trouble."

Emma opened her mouth but the guy lunged her way. He reached out a bear-sized paw, grabbed her waist, and bent as he yanked her forward. Her bag was torn from her grasp as the world turned upside down when her feet were jerked off the floor. He straightened with her hanging over one of his broad shoulders and fisted her bag in his other hand.

"She was never here, Peva. Make sure everyone knows that if anyone comes looking for her. The Vampires might send a human to snoop, since I doubt they'd have the balls to step into Howl unless they're certain she's here. I'll be heading to my den—but keep that between us." He spun, stomping toward the back of the shop. "Fucking bloodsuckers. I hate those bastards."

Chapter Two

Emma kept silent for as long as possible. The guy wasn't even breathing hard despite lugging her through the woods for at least a few miles. They'd traveled up a narrow dirt trail and even sloshed through a shallow stream. They'd entered thickly grown woods with no sign of civilization after exiting the water.

"Um…Mr. Tall and Grim? Can you put me down? I know how to walk."

"Shut up," he growled. "Do you know what I am?"

"Irritated?"

He adjusted his arm over the back of her thighs but didn't stop walking. "Very. That wasn't my question though, and I think you know it. I'm in no mood for jokes."

"I'm sorry."

He kept walking.

"You're a VampLycan. Half Vampire and Lycanthrope."

That slightly slowed his pace. "And irritated."

"Do you have a name?" She stared at his jean-clad ass. It was a beefy one, filling a pair of faded jeans nicely, and his back was broad. She had become very familiar with it since she'd bumped into it at least a thousand times. "I'm Emma."

"It doesn't matter what your name is. You're just my problem. How long do I have to protect you?"

"I'm not sure."

He grumbled something under his breath.

"What? I didn't catch that."

"Good. My mother taught me not to swear in front of women."

"I'm starting to feel dizzy." She tried to lift her head but failed. He was moving too fast. "Plus, I'm getting a headache from having all the blood rush to my brain. *Please* put me down."

He kept walking.

"Pretty please with sugar on top?"

He stopped so fast her face smashed into his back and he bent, really making her dizzy as he set her on her feet. He backed up as she straightened. The world spun and she nearly fell on her ass. He dropped her bag and clamped two big hands on her hips to hold her steady. She had to blink a few times to be able to see anything besides spots.

The guy looked really put out as he glared at her from his superior height. He said nothing, just expressing his bad temper on his features while keeping ahold of her.

"Thanks."

"Aren't you afraid of me?"

She studied him. Seeing someone that deeply tan was rare after living with her grandfather for so long. His features were a bit savage but overall attractive. He parted his lips and she saw sharp fangs. She was also certain he'd shown those to her on purpose, just to appear more frightening.

"No. Should I be?"

"Yes."

"Are you going to hurt me?"

"No."

"Then what's to fear?"

That baffled look on his face was worth the headache she hoped would fade quickly once her body adjusted to being upright again.

"Me."

"You just said you wouldn't hurt me."

"You're human." He sniffed. "Very much so. I'm not, and you know it."

"I was raised by a Vampire." She frowned. "I'm kind of over the *other* thing. VampLycans have a reputation of being honorable. My grandfather trusted your kind without question. I trust *him*. Therefore, it's not that much of a stretch to trust *you*. So no, I'm not afraid of you. You'd have let that woman make the call for someone to put me six feet under if you planned to take me out."

He grimaced. "We don't really kill humans. She was messing with you. Your grandfather raised you? I'm sorry."

"He's a great guy. There's nothing to apologize for."

He gripped her chin with a big calloused hand, turning her head from side to side. "I don't see the scars. I take it he was careful not to leave any."

"He rarely bit me." She frowned. "Rarely as in, I can only remember three times. I wasn't his food source. I'm his granddaughter."

"Three times too many."

Anger surged and she jerked away from his hold. She lifted her hand and held up a finger. "The first time was when we were on the run in the mountains and it was so cold all the animals were gone from the area. He needed enough blood to make sure we both survived. He carried me for a ton of miles, three nights in a row, by the way." She added another finger. "The second time was when we lived in a city and some Vamps grew suspicious of us. He bit me so they could see the marks, to fool them into thinking I was a blood slave when they came for a visit. They don't like humans and Vamps living together otherwise, and he sure couldn't tell them we were related." She lifted a third finger. "Then there was four days ago, when we were surrounded, and he did it again to fool them into thinking I was his slave. I'm not his food source. He *loves* me."

He arched one eyebrow. "Fine. He's a saintly bloodsucker. That's pretty rare. Why are they after you? Why do you need to be protected?"

"My grandpa broke away from his own nest to save me. They've been searching for us ever since."

"What's the whole story?" He crossed his arms. "I deserve to know what I've gotten into."

She hesitated. "My mother was like you...a VampLycan. My grandfather put her and a few others like her in safe locations after they left Alaska. Not everyone remained here when the Werewolves decided the first-generation VampLycans didn't need them sticking around."

"That's not true."

"What part?" She cocked her head, staring at him. "That Werewolves left after the first of your kind hit their teens and started taking over? Or that the packs felt unwelcome here?"

"All VampLycans stayed."

"You're wrong. My mother didn't. And there were a few more like her who wanted to stick with their mothers in a pack, but that didn't work out well. I guess within a year or so, they parted ways. It was a dominance thing, making the packs confused on who to follow. My grandfather found them what he thought would be a safe place in a tiny community outside of a much larger city. He looked out for them...until Vampires attacked one night."

The big guy in front of her scowled. "Why would he care?"

"My mother was his daughter, and the others were VampLycans he'd known since their births. He wanted to protect them. He chose to save me rather than just allow me to die when the Vampires came after my mother and the other VampLycans. His nest went against his orders to leave us in peace, and they brought in another nest to overwhelm them with sheer numbers."

"What about your mother?"

"She knew she couldn't fight them all off with me in her arms. The risk was too great that I'd die. I was only four. She created a diversion instead that allowed my grandfather enough time to get me to safety. He was older than all the other Vampires and could outrun them with me in his arms. Plus, he wasn't their target."

His features softened. "I'm sorry. I take it she didn't make it?"

"No." The pain always existed for Emma when remembering her mother. "She and the other three VampLycans never showed up at the mountain retreat my grandfather owned. That was where they'd always planned to go if anything happened. We waited for two years, until his nest got too close searching for us, before we moved on. She'd have come if she'd survived. We had hope at first that she had escaped without me burdening her."

He sniffed again. "You smell completely human."

"My father was one, but I have a few special traits."

Skepticism widened his eyes. "What kind? You're small and look very weak."

"Wow. That wasn't insulting at all." She scowled.

He frowned back. "I didn't mean it that way."

Emma wanted to snort but refrained, considering she needed his help. "I don't transform or anything. I can see better than normal people do at night. My hearing is keener than average and I'm stronger than a typical human. I also heal way faster than a human does. It was hell hiding those things in school."

"You went to school?"

"I needed an education. Grandpa sent me to school."

He gawked a little. "With humans?"

"Who else? Ever heard of a special school that accepts someone like me? I was really young when I lost my mother."

His gaze lowered down her body. "What other traits did you inherit?" He suddenly bit his finger and grabbed her jaw with his other hand. He waved the bleeding digit beneath her nose. "Smell the blood? Open your damn mouth."

Shock over his actions made it fall open, more than his command. He bent, peered inside. "No fangs protruding." He glanced up at the sky before studying her bare arms. He released her. "You're not burning from the sun."

"I don't have any Vampire traits, besides the quick healing. I could have gotten that from the Werewolf side though."

"Stop calling us that. We're part Lycan."

Emma made a mental note. "Sorry. I didn't mean to insult you. Grandpa said you guys like the older term for what you are. I'll try to remember. Anyway, I heal faster. I broke my arm in two places when I was seven. The doctor said I'd be in a cast for months. Grandpa took me in for a checkup two weeks later and the doctor nearly had a fit when he discovered the breaks had completely healed. Grandpa had to order him to remove the cast, and then wipe his memory of ever meeting me."

"Do you grow fur at all?"

"No. I said I don't transform."

He caught her hand next, examining the tips of her fingers. She allowed it. She'd be staying with him and figured he had a right to know what he was getting into. It would be a good assumption he'd have to worry about his neck if she had Vampire traits. Most of them were horrible creatures who tended to bite into anything alive. Her grandfather was an exception. He was a powerful master, created by someone thousands of years old, and in control of his urges.

"I don't have claws."

He released her hand. "Do you have any more traits?"

She hesitated. "I'm forty years old."

Shock paled his features. "You appear half that."

"I'm aging slower. It's a bitch getting carded at bars, especially since fake IDs are getting more difficult to obtain with modern technology."

He made a soft growl sound. "I'm aware."

"You have that problem too? How old are you?" She didn't notice any wrinkles on his face. He appeared about thirty at most but looks were deceiving with *other* beings. He could be pushing a hundred or two. Her grandfather was over four centuries old but he got carded buying his cigars. Of course, her grandfather would never age in looks. VampLycans did, but it was much slower pace than humans unless their Vampire traits were unusually strong.

"Older than you." He glanced around the woods. "Let's go. It will be dark in an hour and I want you inside."

"The Vamps won't be able to track me here. I was careful, used fake IDs, paid for everything in cash, and followed my grandfather's plan. He's very smart."

He snorted. "I don't trust Vampires, even that one. My father and he were friends, but it's been eighty years since they've had contact. Things and people change."

"I'm sorry about your dad."

He lifted her bag and gripped her arm. "Move."

"Did he die of old age? Grandpa never said if he was a VampLycan or a Lycanthrope."

That question earned her a warning snarl. "He died in battle. And we're called Lycans. Not Lycanthropes. Stop using that term too. Walk or I will carry you."

"Fine." She tried to keep pace with his much longer strides. "You're at war? With what?"

"Not anymore, but there was a time when we had issues with another VampLycan clan."

She let that sink in. "There's more than one?"

"Four. Enough questions."

The spot he was taking her to came into view and she grimaced. It reminded her of one of those old mud homes she'd read about in history books. It was a rounded mound of dirt with grass and bushes covering what would pass for the roof. The only sign that it wasn't just a small hill of dirt was the metal door hidden under part of the overhanging branches. He unlocked the thick door with a combination lock, similar to those on an old bank safe, and threw it open.

Instead of furniture, the room stood empty except for a large metal hatch in the center of the dirt floor. She paused at the entrance.

"Do you need to be carried?"

"You live underground?"

"Yes."

"Shit. You have an actual den? I'm guessing your Lycan traits are more prominent. Please tell me you have indoor plumbing."

"*Move*."

She entered the structure, hoping it didn't collapse around her. Being buried alive didn't sound like a great way to die. The smell of dirt hung heavy inside since the walls, ceiling, and floor were made of it, and he slammed the door behind them, throwing bolts. Some loose soil rained down from above. She turned, having to use her night vision to even make out his shadow since no sunlight penetrated the interior.

"No windows?"

"No. From the sky, this just looks like part of the ground." He gripped her arm. "Can you see at all?"

"Not really. It's pitch dark and you're just a deeper shadow."

"Fuck." He sighed.

His shoulder hit her belly. The world turned upside down and she gasped over finding herself being carried once more. "You suck."

"Shut up."

He bent, the sound of metal creaked, and she assumed he had opened the floor hatch. Then he moved again, and she nearly fell off his shoulder as he proceeded to climb down. Part of her body bumped against the edge of the opening.

His feet made loud thuds on the metal and something slammed overhead. More bolts slid, sealing them inside. Some of the dirt smell faded. He carried her down at least twenty steps into deeper darkness. The chill became more noticeable as they went, and then he paused to open yet another door, sliding more bolts when it closed.

Lights blinded her when he turned them on.

She twisted her head to stare at the furniture. The room wasn't big, only about ten feet by twenty, but it had a couch. A coffee table was placed in front of it, and as he dropped her back onto her feet, she got a better view.

Her gaze took it all in, saw the walls, and she swallowed hard. "Is this one of those old shipping containers? There's enough air in here, right? We're not going to suffocate?"

"There are air vents."

"It's a metal box." Claustrophobia clawed at her. "It's like a big coffin."

He gripped her jaw. She had to turn her body to avoid having her neck painfully twisted. He bent enough to go nose to nose with her.

"This is my safe place. Bloodsuckers can't breach it. We're over twenty-three feet below ground from the roof and the lining of this den is thick. They can't detect body heat at this depth. It also shields us from the GarLycans." He let her go and stepped back.

"The what?"

He frowned. "GarLycans."

"I have no idea what those are. I've never heard of them."

"Gargoyle and Lycan mixed."

Her mouth dropped open. "No shit? Gargoyles are real? Grandpa never mentioned them."

Irritation stamped his features. "They exist. We aren't at war with them, but we once worried it might happen."

Emma let that information sink in. "What do Gargoyles look like?"

He snarled under his breath. "Unbelievable."

"I was just asking. You don't have to get bent out of shape. You grabbing my jaw is getting annoying too. Could you please stop doing that?"

He threw her bag on the couch. "There is your bed. Don't try to leave." He spun around and stomped into the small kitchenette. "I'm hungry. You eat meat, don't you? You're shit out of luck if you don't. It's all I have. I wasn't expecting company."

"Only if you cook it." She was afraid he'd say that he didn't. She'd barf if he handed her raw meat, especially if it was still moving.

He banged around the tiny kitchen. She spotted a full-sized fridge and felt grateful there was electricity inside the metal box. She turned her back on him, staring at the walls, ceiling, and floor. More details sank in. Her best guess was that once it had been some kind of large railway shipping container that he'd somehow managed to relocate into the middle of the woods. It had to have been a lot of effort to dig the hole to dump the thing into.

She hugged her middle and wondered how her grandfather was going to find her buried so deep in the earth. A shiver ran down her spine.

Red peered at the human casually studying his coffee table. Emma bent, touching the smooth stones he'd handpicked to create the top of it. He studied her form. She was a small thing and smelled completely human. She had also become his problem. He bit back a growl.

Cavasia would have a fit when she heard he'd taken off with a woman. He'd spotted a few of the clan on his way out of town and figured it was a good thing he didn't get cell reception inside his den. There would be gossip. It would reach the other clans, and her.

So much for their discussion three months before about possibly living together. She'd be furious over him sharing space with someone else.

A human.

She might be part VampLycan, but it was so minimal that he couldn't detect it by scent. He ran his tongue over his teeth as he pulled out steaks from the small fridge, slapped them into a large pan, and lit a fire beneath it. He could taste her, but she'd probably freak out if he bit into her to get a blood sample.

His father had raised him on battle stories about Malachi, the bloodsucker with a soul. He'd been one of the few Vampires who had refused to kill Lycans when the war broke out. Malachi had loved one enough to take their side. That Vampire helped the pack flee, and protected the women and children during the night hours.

He'd also fathered five children with the Lycan he'd taken as his companion and, according to Emma, her mother had been one of those offspring.

"You haven't mentioned your father. What about him?"

She gazed at him. "I never met him. He and my mom weren't together long. Grandpa said she didn't want to put him at risk of discovering the truth."

"Why did she decide to have you? Was her pregnancy an accident?"

She shot him a dirty look. "No. I wasn't a 'whoops' baby. Mom wanted me. She knew her chances of finding a mate were slim to none, living with humans, and the only VampLycan male in our community wasn't right for her. She met my father and decided to have a baby."

He cleared his throat. "Where is your other family?"

Emma straightened up and her expression smoothed out. "It's just my grandfather and I."

He sealed his lips, not sure if she was aware of her aunts and uncles. His father had said some of Malachi's children with his pureblood Lycan companion had become a danger to the clan. Their Vamp blood had come through stronger than their Lycan mother's, and they'd chosen to live with nests when they'd reached adulthood. Emma's mother must have taken after the Lycan side, if her father had tried to protect her. Malachi had told his father that his woman had died, the last time they'd been in contact.

He racked his brain for more information as he flipped the steaks. The smell made his belly rumble but he ignored it. His father had sworn a blood oath to the Vamp in thanks for helping the Lycans flee when the Vampires betrayed them and declared war. Malachi had stayed with them while they'd structured their new lives in Alaska.

Now that debt was left to Redson to repay. Malachi had also been a father figure to a lot of the first-generation VampLycan children, and had taught them how to fight.

Worry ate at him as he wondered if Peva would decide to tell their clan leader about Emma. Uncle Velder wouldn't be happy about having her in their territory, and less thrilled with the fact that she was being sought by Vampires. It was doubtful that they'd launch a full-scale assault on Howl, but it depended on how badly they wanted to get Emma. The Vampires would lose, but some VampLycan lives could be lost if enough of them attacked at once.

"Why do the Vamps hunt you?"

She bit her lip. "I think mostly my grandfather's old nest wants him to pay for abandoning them. He saved me instead of staying with them. His oldest Vampire really took it personal. My death would be the ultimate revenge."

"Why?"

"Why did they take it personal? I think it's mostly Eduardo's fault. He was second in command and now leads them. He's kind of a prick. Grandpa said he was jealous of my mom and the other VampLycans, always being a big pain in the ass over the nest coming second in priority instead of first."

Dread filled Red. "Your grandfather chose you and your mother over his blooded children?"

"*I'm* his blood." She frowned. "He made Eduardo by turning him into a Vampire. My grandpa ordered him not to attack the community my mother lived in but he did it anyway. Eduardo talked the other Vampires into defying Grandpa and reached out to a large city nest to help him with the attack. My grandpa was nice enough to take in strays…and that's how they repaid him. Eduardo deserves to get his head ripped off for disobeying a direct order."

"Malachi took in strays?"

"Most masters create their own nests with Vampires they personally turned. Grandpa wasn't into doing that. He'd collect the ones other masters had abandoned or who no longer had a master, since some of those guys go nuts. He told me really old Vamps sometimes commit suicide after living longer than they ever wanted to. The world changes too much around them, they grow depressed. Game over by meeting the sun. The Vampire children they made are left behind like orphans. Not all of them are leader types. Grandpa would occasionally take them in. There's security in numbers. Some are mistaken for rogues by the council and killed on sight otherwise. Belonging to a nest is protection. Eduardo was the only one he made. He felt bad for Eduardo."

"Bad?"

"He pitied him. My grandfather had hired him about a hundred years ago to do chores during the day, and one night he woke to find Eduardo severely beaten in the yard, stabbed and dying. Some humans who lived nearby had done it. Eduardo was kind of quiet and shy. He didn't have any friends. I guess they targeted him because of that. Grandpa turned him to give him a second chance at life, and that's when he actually started taking in strays. To give Eduardo a kind of family and friends by making a nest. Then the bastard repaid him by getting pissed because he wasn't Grandpa's favorite. Jackass."

"How could you live with a Vampire and not understand their ways? It would be a great insult to have their master turn his back on them for anyone outside their own kind. The master of a nest chooses loyalty to those under his protection, at all costs."

"My mom, Kallie, was with my grandpa longer. Eduardo knew the score from night one, since the moment he was turned. We were under his protection too." She shrugged. "Eduardo's definitely butt hurt, but he did defy my grandpa. Don't forget that—because *we* haven't. He's been tracking us for thirty-six years. The asshat needs to get over it already."

Her choice of words made Red smile, and he lowered his head, allowing his hair to fall forward and hide his face. He flipped the steaks again, not wanting to burn hers. She'd probably cry or complain.

That killed his humor. He was cooking for a woman in his den. It was an intimate gesture in his culture, usually something men did for serious lovers or mates.

"That smells really good."

He glanced up and noticed she'd moved closer. Her bright blue eyes were startling against her pale features and dark brown hair. She looked elfish and cute.

His cock stirred inside his jeans and he growled when he glanced at the generous swells of her breasts. *No way.*

"Is that insulting or something?" She arched her eyebrows. "I said it smelled good. There's no reason to get testy."

He forced his gaze down to the pan. "It's not that."

She backed up. "Is that better? Are you into personal space while you're near food? You won't snap at me or anything, will you?"

Christ. He was responsible for her, and the idea of spending a lot of time with someone who interested his dick wasn't good. "I'm not a dog."

"I didn't say that you were."

"Aggressive dogs do that when you get too close to their food." He saw the pink in her cheeks. He narrowed his eyes, and he knew that's *exactly* what she'd been thinking. She could deny it all she wanted but she was a terrible liar. "You're a woman, so you need to keep your distance from me."

Her lips parted into an O shape and she backed up more. She glanced at his chest, seeming to assess it. Her gaze jerked back up to his face, and she swallowed hard when her lips sealed.

"I won't attack you."

"Good thing. You're pretty big, and I imagine really strong since you carried me for miles without breaking a sweat or panting."

"Is that another dog joke?" His anger stirred. "This *mutt* is going to protect you. Keep that in mind."

"Hey, I'm not insulting you. Calm down, Sparky."

He dropped the tongs and turned off the flame under the pan, stepping toward her. That insulting name pushed him too far, and he only paused when terror flashed in her blue gaze. She backed away, hitting the door with her ass.

"I had a life until you arrived. Remember that, Emma. I had to drop everything to bring you here. *Stop* insulting me."

"I'm sorry."

She hugged her chest and it made him feel like a total bastard, seeing her trying to make her body appear smaller as she huddled where she stood.

"I sometimes say shit before I think it through. It was kind of a joke."

"Do you see me laughing? You have no idea what kind of shit-storm I'm going to face over having you here."

"Will you lose your job or something? I have money." She relaxed her arms and pointed to her backpack. "There's over ten grand in cash inside my bag, plus some change. I can pay you to keep me here until my grandfather comes, and I have access to more money if that's not enough."

He felt insulted again as he put space between them. "I have my own money. It's not that."

She took a shaky breath. "What is it?"

He hesitated. "I didn't get permission from my clan leader to let you stay in our territory...and there's a woman who's going to be angry that you're inside my den."

"Oh." She lowered her hand to her side, rubbing her jeans nervously. "You have a mate?"

"No, but there's a woman I've talked to about living with me. It's a possible commitment."

Confusion crossed her face. "That sounds like a girlfriend."

He hesitated. "You know nothing about our culture, do you?"

"Just what my grandfather told me. You're half Lycan and Vampire. I know you live in a group you call a clan, and that most of the residents in this town are like you. I know what you can do, such as shifting."

"There are four clans in this area." He ambled back into the kitchen and removed plates from the cupboard. "Everyone in Howl is like me, except for a few mates. I haven't found mine yet, but sometimes a couple will live together to avoid loneliness."

She didn't respond, and when he glanced at her, she stared at the floor. He shrugged it off and put a steak on a plate for her.

"Eat."

Chapter Three

Emma tried to get comfortable on the couch but it wasn't easy. The thing wasn't that long. She might be short but her feet still dangled over the end of it if she didn't curl into a ball. It was cold, too, the blanket insufficient. She tried not to feel as if she were trapped inside a big ol' coffin. The irony wasn't lost on her. She'd lived with a Vampire but had never felt so claustrophobic in her entire life.

The soft snore coming from the back of the long room drove her a little nuts. Her host didn't seem to mind the cold temperatures or sleeping buried underground. She'd kill for some fresh air at that moment and figured it would be a lot warmer at night above ground than inside his den.

He'd left a dim nightlight on in the kitchen area to keep it from being pitch black, something she'd appreciated. It was even a little sweet. She doubted he slept with one on when he was alone and knew it had to be for her benefit.

Dinner had been a silent one. He'd refused to chat, other than telling her his name, and then he'd gone to bed.

What kind of name is Redson? Who'd strap their kid with that? She sighed, rolled trying to get comfortable, and shivered. The cold seemed to seep right into her bones and made them ache. *Maybe that's why he's in such a bad mood. Redson Redwolf would be a tough tag to be stuck with.*

She wished he was a gentleman and had offered her the bed. She'd glimpsed his sleeping area on the other side of the thin divider wall when she'd used the tiny bathroom. It was a roomy mattress on the floor, a few feet thick, with what appeared to be real fur covers over it. It had looked soft, comfortable, and big enough to fit his long legs.

The bathroom wasn't much bigger than a small closet with a sink, toilet, and shower stall shoved into the cramped space. How someone his size used it stunned her. He probably had to shelf his ass on the sink to aim at the bowl when he peed. That mental image made her smile. If he dropped the soap, he'd knock himself out trying to bend for it or turn into a human pretzel.

At least there's a bathroom. She sighed again and pulled the blanket tighter against her throat. She swore she could see her breath in the air, and she burrowed her face against the thin cotton. It didn't help much, and she put her tongue between her teeth to keep them from chattering.

The snoring finally stopped and the silence grew absolute. She turned against the back of the couch and cuddled into the cushions. It kept her only slightly warmer when she drew her legs up to curl into a tight ball. Her head under the covers also helped, but not by much. *I'll probably catch pneumonia or the cold from hell after this.*

"What is wrong?"

Redson's voice so near made her gasp, and she struggled with the covers to stare up at the dark shape blocking the small light from the kitchen. "What?"

"Your sighing is annoying me and the couch creaks every time you move." Irritation deepened his voice to take on a growling tone. "It woke me."

"I'm freezing. I don't suppose you have a heater, do you?"

He bent. She could smell a masculine, pleasant scent. His fingertips brushed her cheek. "Damn. Your skin is chilled."

"Sorry."

It stunned her when his hands dug under her body and he lifted her, blanket and all, off the couch. She couldn't even grab at him with her limbs tangled in the bedding.

She realized when he turned into the light that he was bare chested. He frowned as she stared at him.

"You are too human. Your Lycan blood should keep you warm but you feel cool to the touch. Are you sure you're not more Vampire than you claim?"

"No. The cold wouldn't bother my grandpa much. It does me."

He walked past the kitchen, into the area he used for his room, and dropped to his knees. The fall made her gasp again but he didn't drop her. Instead, he lay her gently down on something really soft that sank under her weight as he pulled his arms from under her back and thighs.

"Roll over and get under my blankets." He tore off the one he'd given her for the couch.

She rolled. Though it was too dark to see much in that area of his den, the soft feel of thick fur meant he was giving her the bed. "Thank you."

She wiggled into pure heaven. His body had made the bed toasty warm under the fur blanket, and she discovered soft sheets beneath it. His pillow was the body-length type, super soft too, and she tried to ignore the fact that she just wore a pair of underwear with a nightshirt.

She'd refused to sleep in a bra or her jeans. She'd shucked them both after he'd disappeared to sleep. He'd probably noticed that, with his superior vision, when he'd taken the blanket.

"Scoot over."

Her eyes widened. "What?"

"Make room for me." He sounded irritated. "You need my body heat to keep you warm."

"I think I'll be okay with the fur. It's real, isn't it?" *Shit. I shouldn't have asked that.* She imagined little bunnies giving up their lives to make it—a bunch of them. Guilt hit her over that concept. "Never mind. I don't want to know."

"It's not real fur."

He pushed at her. Cold air blasted her body as he lifted the covers she'd burrowed under and his big warm body pressed against hers as he forced her to move. It was that or be crushed. She rolled over to get out of his way.

She tried to keep space between them but his weight dipped the mattress. It made her fall back into him as he settled, and her hand touched bare skin. She patted a sprinkling of hair before jerking her hand away.

"Tell me that's not your junk."

"My leg."

Her hands fisted her shirt over her stomach and she realized one of her legs pressed against his. "You don't have pants on!"

"No. I sleep bare."

Oh shit. I'm in bed with a naked guy. "Tell me you've got boxers on or something."

"Fine. I have them on. Now go to sleep. Are you warm enough?"

"Yes." She paused. "You're lying to me, aren't you?"

He hesitated too. "The fur is real."

"I meant about wearing something."

"I'm flat on my back and you're on your side, facing away. Just don't turn over and place your hands on me."

Her heart hammered inside her chest.

"The animals didn't suffer."

"What?" She was thinking about being in bed with a stranger, sans his clothes.

"The fur came from my meals. It was either throw their pelts away or put them to use. I realize it might offend your human side but it's warm, isn't it?"

"Just tell me it's not cute little bunnies." The topic helped distract her from the fact he didn't have anything on.

"No bunnies." He chuckled. "They *are* annoying though. Rabbits invade my garden and eat everything. They're pests."

"Let me guess. As a kid, you didn't get a visit from the Easter Bunny. You'd love them if you had. Didn't you at least see any of those adorable cartoons made about him?"

The mattress shifted a little as Redson spoke. "You *did*?"

"Of course."

"Before your mother died?"

"Before and after."

For several moments, the only sound in the room was their breathing. He finally spoke. "The Vampire celebrated human holidays for you?"

"Yes." Worry hit Emma suddenly, and tears filled her eyes. "I hope my grandpa's okay. He's not bad—and I don't like the way you call him 'the Vampire'. His name is Malachi, and he's the best grandpa ever. You can even call him Mal for short. That's what he tells humans. His name is kind of old fashioned and he didn't want to raise suspicion."

The mattress shifted slightly again and warm breath fanned her cheek. "Tell me about him."

She smiled in the darkness. "He's funny, and he tries to give me as normal a life as he can. You know, minus the picnics in the park on sunny days."

"How old did you say you were when you were separated from your mother?"

"Four."

"How did he care for you while he slept?"

She hesitated. "He made sure I was locked in, to keep me from wandering away, and he slept in the same room so I could see him. It made me less afraid, knowing he was there. He's old and powerful enough to be able to wake easily even during daylight hours. We adjusted. I started sleeping during the daytime after a few months, until starting school. Kids are astonishingly flexible."

"He locked you in?"

"I was a little kid. He needed to keep me close and safe. Can you imagine what would have happened if I'd gone outside to play in the sunshine and gotten hurt? He couldn't get to me until the sun went down without being burned. Then he would have been hurt and hungry. That might have ended in tragedy. We lived alone, meaning I was the only blood source nearby. Figure it out. He didn't want to risk ever accidentally hurting me. You know they can get kind of insane when they're severely injured and starved. He might have gone after my blood to heal himself without meaning to."

"You said you went to school. How did he manage that?"

"He hired two nannies who pretended to be my aunts. He'd taught me enough that I was able to start school in the first grade with human kids. One of the nannies would come in before dawn. She thought he left to go to work early. She'd take me to school and another one would pick me up. That one thought he worked until evening. That way, I always had someone to attend conferences with my teachers or come get me if there was an emergency. They went along with it because he smoothed things over with his ability to control minds if they ever suspected anything was off about the arrangement."

"What kind of emergency?"

"Like when I fell off the swings and broke my arm in two places. The school called one of my nannies to get me. Later, when I hit junior high, he just had a housekeeper in our home during the day, to be there if I needed something while he slept. I could walk to and from school by myself." She turned her head but couldn't make out his face. The dividing wall totally blocked the nightlight but she could see the deeper shadow that outlined his head inches from her own. "He did the best he could, and I think I turned out pretty well."

"But you need my protection."

He didn't say it, but he implied her grandfather had failed her somehow. "And he sent me somewhere safe, didn't he? That's part of looking out for me. You said you'd protect me. He stayed behind to give me time to escape. The Vamps had surrounded our home too quickly for us to flee together, and that's the *only* reason I'm here. He'll come for me as soon as it's safe."

"How many other times has he had to send you to a stranger for protection?"

Anger stirred at the thought that he was insulting her grandpa. She rolled a little to face him more. "This is the first. I've never been away from him except for a few times, but those weren't because I was in danger."

"When?"

She hesitated. "I went to college and lived on campus. I dated sometimes. I'm not a forty-year-old virgin spinster who's a shut-in with my grandfather. Don't make my life sound pathetic. I have a good one."

He said nothing for a long time and exhaustion tugged at her. She was finally warm and comfortable, the stress of traveling behind her. She *did* feel safe with Redson. He growled a lot but he'd taken her into his den. It might be a box in the ground but it would take a hell of a lot for someone or something to reach them. He owned a buried fortress.

"Why would he send you here now? Was it only because he couldn't flee with you?"

She hated how tight her chest felt. "I don't want to talk about it."

"Emma." His tone implied he wasn't about to let it drop.

"We had a safe house near the one we lived in, but he said 'last resort' to me. That was our code for me to come here. I had a lot of time to think while I was traveling to Alaska, and I'm sure he didn't want me to go to our safe house in case he couldn't get away from all those Vampires. They could have tortured my location out of him. But even Eduardo would hesitate to come after me in VampLycan territory."

"How many?" He growled the question.

"How many what? Vampires that showed up?"

"How many lovers had you had?"

The abrupt change of topic shocked her. "What?"

"How many lovers have you accepted into your bed?"

"I'm not answering that unless you do."

She smirked, figuring that would end the conversation…and she was right as the silence stretched. She closed her eyes and began to drift to sleep.

"Twelve."

The number surprised her. She figured Lycans, even half-breed ones, would chase a lot of tail. The fact that he was half Vampire also should have meant a string of lovers left behind. Vamps loved sex while feeding. She knew way too much about her grandfather's habits after growing up with him. He'd had a lot of women spend the night to keep himself fed.

"How many?"

She bit her lip, opened her eyes to the darkness, and sighed. "Two."

The silence stretched again, and she relaxed.

"Why only two?"

Her teeth clenched. "Why only twelve? You're older than I am, and a guy."

"I'm picky about who I touch, and I don't travel far from home."

"Small town, slim pickings," she guessed aloud.

He softly growled. "Wrong. I don't touch the ones in my clan. One day I may find my mate, and I don't want to make the mistake of causing her pain."

Interest sparked. "How would that hurt a potential mate?"

"Would you enjoy living in a town where a bunch of the women had slept with your mate?"

Put that way, she could understand. It was quite sweet that Redson would consider the feelings of someone he'd never met before. The big guy was full of surprises. "So you only slept with ones who didn't live in town?"

"Yes. I was never attracted to any unmated women in my clan."

"That woman in the store was beautiful."

"It's not a matter of beauty. My clan is a close-knit one. The women feel more like family to me than potential mates. We don't get many females who travel to Howl who aren't already mated, but the ones who do are potential mates I've tested compatibility with."

"What about this girlfriend of yours?" She was curious about the woman.

"She's not my girlfriend by human definition. She travels this way to see family who are a part of my clan, and we enjoy sex together. We're both lonely and have been discussing sharing a home."

"How do you know when you find your mate? My grandfather didn't tell me that much about Werewolves. I know Vampires fall in lust, usually it results in obsession, and they often take companions."

"Lycans, not Werewolves," he corrected. "You avoided answering my question. Why only two?"

She hesitated. "I have shitty taste in men. Two big mistakes were more than enough. I've learned my lesson."

The mattress moved as he shifted his position on the bed again. His hot breath fanned her neck and his leg rubbed against hers. She guessed he'd turned fully on his side to face her and was proven right when he spoke.

"Explain. I answered *your* questions. I'm curious, and you did wake me. I don't fall asleep easily."

She sighed. "In high school, I seemed kind of weird to other kids. I couldn't invite them to sleepovers, since no parent would send their daughter to spend the night with someone being raised by my older brother. That's the story we told everyone to explain my grandpa looking so young. He couldn't pretend to be my dad after I hit my teens. He might pass for twenty-six or possibly thirty at most. He needed me with him at night in case we were found. So that meant *I* couldn't go stay over at a friend's home. I didn't have many friends anyway. I had to be secretive to protect my grandpa. I didn't exactly encourage anyone to grow curious about my life. My first boyfriend came along while I was in college. I lived in the dorm for a few months before I met the guy. I thought I fell in love. It turned out he was a douchebag."

"Excuse me?" Shock sounded in his voice.

"It's a derogatory term to call a guy with messed-up morals. I guess I screamed 'virgin,' since I was so shy. He made a bet with his friends that he could nail me. I didn't know he was only pretending to care about me until after I let him take me to bed." Humiliation still burned inside her chest at the memory. "He told all of his friends, they told other people, and I left that school. I thought he loved me. He really made me believe he did…but I was just a way to earn him a few bucks and pats on the back."

"I hear pain in your voice." His tone deepened into a growl.

"It wasn't a breeze being laughed at and snickered over. Some of those girls were flat-out mean. He broke my heart by not being who I thought, and I just went home to Grandpa. He offered to kill the guy but I asked him to leave it alone. I avoided men for a long time."

"You said there were two."

"I was turning thirty, and that's rough on some women. I decided to start going out, to meet guys. I found one but he turned out to be a cheating bastard. He probably would have gotten away with it because he was a skilled liar, but I have a heightened sense of smell. I knew he'd been with another woman. He stood there lying to me with her scent all over him. The bastard hadn't even showered or changed his clothes after he'd banged her."

She remembered her question. "How do you know when you find your mate?"

He hesitated. "It's part attraction, part feelings, and tasting."

That piqued her interest. "Tasting?"

"Supposedly, when we taste their blood we know for sure, but there's strong attraction first."

Her jaw dropped. "You drink blood? I assumed you were more Lycan than Vampire."

"We sometimes bite during sex."

"Oh." She nodded into the darkness. "I got it. You don't need to explain that one to me. I accidently walked in on my grandpa with a woman once. I heard loud noises coming from his room when I came home from band practice and rushed in, thinking he was hurt." She chuckled. "I don't know who was more embarrassed. Probably me. I'm just glad the woman didn't remember it. That would have been really awkward, since Linda lived next door and I saw her all the time until we moved."

"He didn't kill her?"

"My grandpa *isn't* a murderer. He only takes what he needs to survive." She was starting to feel offended. "Whatever you've heard about Vampires, don't apply it to him. He's not some blood-driven fiend who kills his victims. He's old and powerful. The woman next door kept hitting on him. One night he was really hungry, and his defenses were down. One thing led to another. He fed from her, they had sex, and he made her forget. While he was in her head, he told her that she was no longer attracted to him. He's good at that hypnotic stuff. She moved on to date the mailman."

"What did you see when you walked into the bedroom?"

She wrinkled her nose, remembering. "Grandpa had her bent over in front of him while they were going at it. He was taking blood from her neck." She paused. "She didn't seem to mind." She cleared her throat. "That was a sight I wish I could forget. I know my friends think he's very attractive since he looks so young, but to me, he's just…my grandpa."

"That's how VampLycans taste. We bite sometimes during sex but only when the urge strikes. It's rare though, and we never bite each other at the same time or a mating happens during unprotected sex."

She let that sink in. "Why? Do you need the blood?"

"No. If the sex is really good, it's an instinctual thing to bite." He paused. "You must not have many VampLycan traits at all."

"I don't."

"I figured that when you said you'd only had two lovers."

"What's that supposed to mean?"

"You don't go into heat, do you? Lycans are also very sexual. They crave sex. Vampires do too when they feel bloodlust."

His tone didn't sit right with her. "You make it sound like a bad thing, me being so human. I don't want to drink blood or grow a tail. I think I got the best parts. Of course, it has downsides too."

"You can't keep human friends for long."

"Exactly." She remembered all the ones she'd walked away from over the years. "They start to notice I'm not aging the way they do. Plus, I have a grandpa they try to seduce. He swore not to date any of them and has never broken his word."

"He wouldn't take blood from your friends?"

"No."

"Where did he get his blood supply? All from women he dated?"

She hesitated. "He's kind of old fashioned. He hired some house staff to come in a few times a week to clean and run errands. He'd take blood from them. He paid them well, and it wasn't as if they ever knew or remembered. He'd wipe their minds. But he also dated, because he doesn't have sex with the staff."

"He doesn't have a companion?"

"No. I kind of killed that option for him." More guilt filled her. "It's always a risk, if he takes a human one, that she'll betray him. Some would freak out if they realized what he is, or they'd tell someone. He didn't want a blood slave because, let's be real. It would be like dating a robot, and he's not into that. Most Vamps who own blood slaves are egotistical assholes with zero compassion. He values human life. He couldn't allow a Vampire to live in our house because he couldn't trust one to keep her fangs out of me. My living with them would have been too tempting. His property would have been considered hers as his companion."

"Meaning anyone on the staff or living under the same roof is fair game if she wanted to bite them?"

"Pretty much. It's a Vamp thing. They see humans as property if you live in their home. That's not how Grandpa sees me. But a companion would."

Silence stretched between them again, and Emma nearly fell asleep. Until Redson asked, "Have you ever gone into heat?"

The question shocked her. "Um, *no*."

"Are you certain?" His voice deepened.

"I think I'd have noticed."

"Have you only slept with humans?"

"Yes. We avoided other Vampires. They would have been more interested in my neck than my personality. And packs hate Vampires being in their territory. We changed towns if any of them even looked twice at me. Since we're being hunted, we kept away from VampLycans because Grandpa didn't want to put any of you at risk unless he absolutely had to."

"By calling in the blood oath."

"Yes. It was a last resort."

"Have you ever had to run before from his nest?"

"We've had to move plenty of times. I think Grandpa sent me here alone because the Vamps that came to the door were from the Vampire Council. It means Eduardo got them involved. Also, like I said, he was probably worried about torture and giving up the safe-house location."

"The council can contact all nests associated with them to help seek out you and your grandfather."

"I know. It means I needed to go where there were no nests. Grandpa didn't say that, but I figured it out on my own."

Redson sighed. "Sleep, Emma."

She snuggled further under the covers. The warmth felt wonderful, and she tried forgetting she was sleeping with a naked guy. It had been ten years since she'd done that. It wasn't exactly the same situation. She'd been romantically involved with that boyfriend.

The idea of having sex with Redson seemed kind of scary. He looked rough and wasn't all human. He also had a tendency to be very physical. He just scooped her into his arms whenever he wanted, without permission.

Would he be that kind of lover? Just grab me and take what he wants, when he wants it?

The concept was oddly appealing.

What am I thinking? He's not my type. I like tame, suit-wearing soft guys who open doors and say pretty words. She sincerely doubted Redson owned much more than faded jeans. He was too down to earth to care about appearances. So far his social skills were lacking too.

Life with her grandfather had given her high expectations. A lot could be said for being raised by a Vampire over four hundred years old. He opened doors for women, had impeccable manners when he wished, and had raised her to appreciate a gentleman. That certainly wouldn't be the VampLycan lying in bed next to her.

Redson has fangs and he growls…he's too gruff. He also has a girlfriend, she reminded herself. *Although*, she reasoned, *he did say she wasn't really a girlfriend*. They'd considered living together until he found his mate.

Another thought entered her mind. *Who is his mate?*

Don't even think about him that way, she ordered. It would be a heartbreak waiting to happen if she fell for him. That was a complication she didn't need. Life had been full of disappointments and pain already.

Redson wasn't human. Even if they fell in love, a VampLycan woman could come along and nature would demand he be with her if they were mates.

Chapter Four

Red woke with a raging hard-on and Emma's scent torturing him.

He didn't move as he silently evaluated the situation. She'd turned in her sleep to face him and was snug against his side. Only thin material separated her lush breast from his chest. Her head rested on his shoulder and somehow his arm had wound around her back. Each of her breaths teased his throat, her mouth close enough to kiss.

His cock throbbed, straining against the bedding. One of her thighs rested over the top of his, achingly close to his dick. Her leg stretched down part of the length of his, her heel near his calf. It was a reminder that he was a lot taller and bigger than her.

The shirt she wore must have ridden up because her soft belly was bare against his side, skin to skin. One of her hands rested on his lower stomach—again, too close to his dick for comfort.

It would be easy to roll, pin her under him, and fist her underwear. One tug and they'd be gone, with nothing stopping him from taking her. He could be inside her before she even woke.

His dick throbbed harder, a heartbeat below his waist. Her size made him hesitate—not to mention the fact she was mostly human. She might not welcome him fucking her... but she *was* in his bed, inside his territory, and snug against him. Sure, he'd put her there, but she was the one who'd curled into him.

FUCK!

He snarled and forced her off him. He rolled away. The air was chilly after being under the blankets with shared body heat. He heard her breathing change as he rose to his feet, happy she'd admitted she couldn't see as well as he could in the dark. Otherwise when he stormed to the bathroom, she'd have seen his dick sticking straight out.

He closed the door and wished for a lock, not that he thought she'd follow him inside the cramped confines. He didn't bother with a light; he knew every inch of his den too well. He squeezed the shaft of his dick with one hand to find some relief from the immediate ache, as he used his other to yank open the mirror and locate lube.

He kept a tube it for emergencies—and this was a big one. Otherwise his houseguest was going to be fucked, in every sense. On her back, bent over in front of him, against a wall...he wished she were pinned there now so he could take while standing. She'd feel a hell of a lot better than his hand.

He coated his dick, the cold gel barely easing the hot need, and furiously pumped his hand with his head tilted back. He clenched his teeth to prevent making any sounds and let his imagination go wild.

Emma naked, spread open for him and in heat. Hell, he could dream. Nothing was hotter than a woman whimpering and clawing at a man to fuck her for hours. Her pussy would be soaking wet, hot, and swollen.

He imagined trying to work his dick inside her. Passion burned him alive at the thought. He'd have to go slow, maybe coax her into a fever so she wouldn't be afraid when she saw how much he wanted her. He bet those humans she'd fucked had nothing on him.

Imagining her thighs spread and his mouth between them was almost too much. She'd taste so damn good. Sweet honey that he could lick until she was begging him to fuck her. He would, too. Slow at first, until she adjusted to his size, and then hard and fast.

His balls tightened, and he couldn't hold back the groan as he came in a rush. It might have been embarrassing how fast it happened but the door was closed. She would never know. His body shook from the force of it, his hips jerking with his dick in hand, and he kept coming until he couldn't take anymore. He released his shaft and grabbed for the shower nozzle.

Cold water made him curse as it blasted him but a few adjustments turned the water warmer. He took his time shaving his face and washing his hair, even brushing his teeth with the shower still running.

He didn't know how he was going to protect a woman when the only current threat to her was *him*—and the fact he wanted to fuck her.

He'd known she'd be trouble the second he spotted Emma. It was those damn pretty blue eyes, that full, pouty little mouth, and how damn helpless she looked. Every protective instinct flared to life when he'd understood who she was and why she was there.

He was sworn to protect her for as long as she was in danger. For the first time, he prayed the bloodsuckers would come and cause some trouble. He'd tear them apart and then send Emma back to wherever the hell she'd come from. It couldn't happen soon enough.

Red lingered after he turned off the water, trying to dry in the tight space. He usually stepped into the bedroom area to do that but he didn't think his guest would appreciate seeing him naked. He wrapped the towel around his waist and opened the door.

The light in the kitchen had been turned on and the bed was empty. He stared at it, stunned.

Emma had made his bed.

It was kind of nice that she'd done that.

The smell of coffee teased his nose, and he was in for another surprise. Movement had him turning his head to find her peering at him from near the fridge. She'd exchanged her T-shirt and panties for a long-sleeved sweatshirt and jeans. Disappointment hit—and he hated it. Because he'd wanted to look at her bare legs.

"Do you mind if I cook us breakfast? You have cans of corned-beef hash and ketchup."

His eyebrows rose. "For breakfast?"

She shrugged. "It's good."

"I usually have it for lunch."

A cute little frown curved her mouth, drawing his attention to it. "You don't have eggs and the only fresh thing you seem to have in the fridge is half a dozen steaks. Were you expecting company?"

He shook his head. "I spend my weekends here in the warm months. I restock every time I come for the next week. I put them in frozen and they slowly thaw inside the fridge. I'm going to have to hit town for more supplies soon."

Another thought struck, and he winced.

"Are you okay?"

She'd noticed. He cleared his throat, holding her gaze. "Do you need any female stuff? You know…woman things? Is that time of the month coming?"

She shook her head. "I don't have periods."

He gaped. "What? You said you were only forty. Humans don't hit that thing until they're older."

"You mean menopause?" Amusement flashed in her blue eyes.

"Yeah. That."

"I live with a Vampire. Bleeding for days every month isn't exactly a smart thing to do. I took care of it some years ago."

Red was horrified. "You had yourself sterilized?"

"No!" She shook her head. "I take a shot every three months instead. I have some, but don't worry. I don't plan to be here that long. I always keep them with me since once a location is blown, we can't ever go back."

"You don't need a doctor to give them to you?"

"Not with my grandpa and his ability to compel people into doing what he wants. He, um, talks doctors into giving me a supply of the shots to go, then wipes their memories. I get a two-year supply when we do it. It's safer that way, rather than having to go through all the paperwork and creating new medical files every few months. I try to leave as little information about myself as possible. I told you…we were being hunted by Eduardo and the other Vampires from his nest."

She couldn't get pregnant.

He felt his dick respond and changed the subject quickly, to prevent the towel wrapped around his waist from rising. There would be no hiding his reaction if he didn't think of something else. "How many Vampires are in this nest?"

She shrugged. "We don't know how many Eduardo is in control of these days. There used to be six in the nest when my grandpa ran things. They can be as small as three Vamps up to dozens. It depends on where they're located, who their master is, and if they're able to support themselves without drawing notice."

"You said they showed up at your home and your grandfather stayed behind? How many did you see?"

She thought back. "At least ten were there. He did tell me through our link that Eduardo hadn't created those Vamps. They were sent from the council. I'm assuming Eduardo just followed them."

"Your link?"

"Um...it's a Vampire thing. I was young when I began living with Grandpa. My mind didn't have any natural defenses yet, and he trained me to pick up and send thoughts."

"You can mentally communicate with him?" The concept stunned him. "Only mates can do that."

"Mates?" Her lips parted. "Ewww! I'm not *mated* to my grandpa."

"*VampLycan* mates can do that," he corrected. "Can you talk to him now?"

"No. It only works in close proximity."

"How close?"

"I don't know. We can talk to each other in the house but he can't send me a thought if I'm at the store, like he forgot to add trash bags to the list or something."

"It's similar to a mated pair on distances. Can you feel what he does?"

"Not really, unless it's a super-strong emotion. I knew he was afraid for a split second before I fled the house, but then it was gone."

"I meant physical sensations. If he's hurt, do you feel the injury?"

"No. Just strong emotions like if he's pissed or scared."

He smiled. "Mates have strong connections. They can send feelings through their bond but also physical responses."

"Really?" She looked surprised.

"Mates are special. They have attributes that humans never will."

"Great," she muttered, turning away. Her voice lowered further. "Another one."

"Another what?"

She softly cursed before turning to face him again. "I forgot your hearing would be as good as my grandfather's. It's just that I'm tired of being treated as if I'm deficient because I'm so normal. At least I can enjoy sunny days without dying and I don't have a tail."

Her feelings were hurt. He could see it in her eyes and hear it in her defensive tone. "I didn't mean it that way."

"Sure." She shrugged. "Whatever. Do you want corned-beef hash or not? Can I cook? I'm always starving when I wake."

"Go ahead. Or give me a few minutes to dress and I'll cook."

"I've got it, Redson." She disappeared out of his sight. "I'm not totally useless," she mumbled.

He knew women were emotional, and he'd somehow just triggered her anger. He softly growled and decided to get dressed. There wasn't a lot of privacy, but she would either watch or not. He turned his back, dropped his towel, and put on his jeans.

Emma refused to slam the pan onto his little cooktop burner, despite her anger. It was a mystery why she'd expected Redson not to view her as a weaker species. Her grandfather had reminded her of that very thing at every opportunity, intentionally or not.

It could be her attraction to Redson, causing that disappointment she suffered. He was massively hot, and taboo on top of it.

She turned around to ask him where he kept his can opener. The sight of him bent, tugging up pants, and his muscular, beefy bare butt muted her.

She spun, moving before she was caught gawking.

Nice ass...and he doesn't wear underwear. She also noted he was tan all over. That led to picturing him sunbathing nude. *Stop*, she ordered her imagination. *He's taken. Off limits. It's a bad idea.* Somewhere there was some VampLycan woman who'd probably claw her eyes out if she didn't stop drooling over the tall hunk.

It was a sobering possibility. She was part VampLycan, but she didn't have their kick-ass abilities. As strong as she was, it wouldn't be anywhere near equal to a full-blooded one. The fight would be a painful joke, not in her favor.

She felt curiosity over the kind of woman Redson would be attracted to. She glanced around surreptitiously, searching for a photo. None were displayed.

The can opener was nowhere to be found. Frustration rose. "Redson?" She turned, hoping he had finished dressing.

She nearly smacked her face against his bare chest.

"What?"

She raised her chin. He was super tall, something she'd forgotten until he was inches away. "Where's the can opener? It's hard to cook anything if I can't get the lids off."

He held out one of those big hands of his. Sharp claws grew from the nail beds as she watched in opened-mouth wonder.

"Right here. Pass them to me."

"That's, um…handy." She took a step back and held up the first can.

He made easy work of it, running the tip of his thumbnail around the rim.

"I hope you washed your hands really good—and your nails, while you were at it."

He arched his eyebrows. "I just showered and washed my hair."

"I'll pretend that was a solid yes." She took it, giving him the second one, and used a fork to scrape out the contents of the can. "I love this stuff."

"Me too."

He stepped closer—and she froze in place when his arms came around her to pour out the second can by roughly tapping the bottom of it. She was trapped between him and the mini stove. Emma turned her head, peering up at him.

"Do you know what personal space is?"

"Do you know that this is my den?"

"Fair enough."

She was grateful for his protection. His father had died; therefore, he technically could have told her she was shit out of luck. Klackan Redwolf had sworn a blood oath to her grandfather. The son didn't have to honor that promise. She didn't want him to regret it by complaining too much.

He grabbed a wooden spoon, stirring the hash as he used his other hand to dump in ketchup. She remained still, watching as he cooked, unsure how to extricate herself from where she stood. She glanced up at him again, noticing he'd shaved. Redson wore some delicious aftershave that was masculine but faint, urging her to get closer to appreciate the smell. She resisted.

"You got rid of the facial hair."

He shrugged. "It grows fast. I remove it every week to avoid growing a long beard. It will look the same as it did within days."

"Do you want me to get plates?" *Good excuse to let me go.*

"You're fine."

That wasn't exactly true. He was so big that she felt a little dwarfed in the circle of his arms. He had no problem looking over her to see the pan. She bit her lip and decided to just be blunt. He'd stated he was considering living with some woman but he was acting as if he were single. Definite "I'm hitting on you" vibes were being sent her way.

"What are you doing?"

"Cooking."

"You know that's not what I'm talking about. I can't move without touching you, and you're doing the cooking after I already offered."

He peered down at her.

"What are you doing?" She spoke softer the second time.

"Cooking."

"You're totally playing stupid, yet I know you're not. What is this?" She glanced at his arms trapping her before looking into his pretty eyes.

That drew a frown from him. "You were in my way, and I didn't want to pick you up. You might have gotten mad since you didn't seem to enjoy that yesterday."

"You could have asked me to step aside, you know."

He shrugged. "I can see and reach around you."

"Redson—"

"Call me Red," he rasped, his voice lowering enough to resemble a sexy growl.

Her heart skipped a beat. A soft click sounded, signaling he'd turned off the flame from under the pan. "Is it done?"

He suddenly surprised her by gripping her hips. She grabbed at his arms for something to cling to and keep her balance but he spun as he lifted her right off her feet. Solid wood bumped her back as he pinned her against the wall.

Red had beautiful eyes. The brown had golden flecks in the irises, their shape exotic, and then the gold turned more yellow, nearly glowing.

It continued until the brown was almost entirely overtaken by the brighter color. Emma couldn't look away for anything. It was amazing and enthralling at the same time.

There was also something alarming about it…something familiar.

"Shit. Don't!" Her mind started working again. "You're going to try to do that thing Vampires do with their eyes." She forced her gaze to his full lips. "I didn't know VampLycans had that ability."

"Look at me."

She shook her head, her hands getting a good grip on his biceps. Red had really hot skin, maybe a trait of his Lycan blood, since Vamps ran a little cool to the touch unless they'd just fed. He had such kissable lips…they looked soft yet firm. She bet he'd be a good kisser if his fangs weren't extended. Then it might get tricky to avoid accidental blood loss if he nicked her with them.

"Emma."

"I don't want to be hypnotized or ordered to do whatever it is you want. That's rude."

"Look at me."

"No way." She continued to stare at his mouth. "Just tell me what you want and don't try to use your special gifts on me."

"I'm not trying to influence you."

"I'm not naïve! I know what happens when eyes glow. My grandpa is a Vamp, remember? I've watched him do it thousands of times, and you wouldn't enjoy my reaction."

"What does that mean?"

"I get killer headaches and might throw up afterward. Grandpa had to sometimes control me, and he thinks I've built a resistance. He can still get in but I pay for it later. I'm sure you don't want me losing whatever's left of last night's dinner on your floor."

Red's lips parted and he growled. "He controlled you? I thought you said he treated you well."

"He does! Sometimes I'd get scared when I was younger, and he'd have to kind of take over for me. I mentioned we lived in the city around other Vamps at one point. Have you ever met a blood slave?"

She glanced up into his gaze, happy to see his eyes no longer glowed golden. A lot of the brown had bled back into them. She felt safe enough to keep eye contact.

"Yes. They're brainless creatures."

"I wouldn't go that far. You're making it sound as if they're zombies. Okay," she quickly amended. "Maybe I see your point. They aren't exactly emotional or independent. They just do as they're told without resistance. Sometimes the local nest would get nosey and spy on us. Grandpa made sure they believed I was his slave."

"Why?"

"He wanted to keep me alive."

"Why would they have cared if you were his blood slave or not?"

"Humans aren't allowed to know about Vampires! It's a *death* sentence. He'd get inside my head and shut me down when they started watching us too closely. He had to make them think I was his blood slave.

But after a while, I started getting sick. We moved to a remote area without other Vamps around because he feared for my health."

Suspicion tensed his features. "You don't know if he fed from you or not when he took away your will."

"It's called trust—and I know without a doubt he wouldn't have taken advantage of me. I'm not *food*. I'm his heart. He couldn't exactly tell them I was his granddaughter. Vamps can tell that he's old and I'm not. Or they might have guessed I'm part VampLycan—and again with the death sentence, since I'm weaker."

"City Vampires still hate VampLycans?"

"I think it's more of a fifty/fifty split between fear and hatred. They know your kind will come after them if they ever try to repeat the past by using Lycans as breeders. But they don't like anyone telling them what they can or can't do, either. They want to avoid another war, but I don't belong to a VampLycan clan. Which means killing me would mean no blowback on them."

"Who said the war ended?"

Her eyebrows arched, studying him. "You're still fighting Vampires in Alaska?"

He hesitated but then shrugged. "We tend to avoid Vampires, but there have been some incidents lately involving another clan being attacked by them. Lycan packs fear us."

"Why do Lycans fear you?"

"Do you remember what your mother looked like when shifted?"

"No."

"We don't resemble wolves. Lycans can pass for a wolf from a distance, but up close they're larger. We're different. The Vampire blood gives us a more humanoid shape. We've got less fur, more mass, and we're stronger." He paused. "Faster. It's a hell of a lot harder to kill us since we heal at a rate they can't, especially if we sink our fangs into whoever we're fighting. Then the Vampire side of us is revealed. A wound will close within seconds while we're feeding. And *all* VampLycans are alphas, unlike Lycans. Packs are built to follow one person or a pair, but not a large group. It confuses their instincts."

She let that information sink in. Another question popped into her head. "You mentioned these GarLycans. What's their story? You don't seem to trust them. Why?"

"How much did your grandfather share with you about our history?"

She thought back. "Vampires and Lycans used to work and live together. He said it was a mutually beneficial arrangement, since Vampires could wipe the memories of any humans who started to look cross-eyed at a Lycan. Lycans could keep Vampires safe while they slept during the day. Life had never been better and everyone was friendly as could be. Grandpa told me each race used to live in tiny groups but once they combined forces, Lycans and Vampires had numbers equal to the humans who lived near them. Mixed-species relationships began, and it was all good…until a Lycan ended up pregnant by a Vampire. Then shit hit the fan. Grandpa said a lot of his people tried to slaughter all the Lycan men, to force the women to becoming baby-makers."

Red smiled. "The way you say things." He sobered. "That's how it went down, though. Vampires attacked the race they'd called friends and allies. Do you know how Lycans fight?"

"I imagine with claws and lots of biting involved."

"They send their breeding-age women and all the children away, with the mated men to protect them. The single men and older members will stand and fight to the death to give them time to flee. Over half the pack stayed to fight to give the rest a chance."

"I didn't know that."

Red nodded. "It's all about protecting future generations and making certain their race survives. The Vampires didn't attack right away. And there wasn't just one woman who was pregnant by a Vampire. There were dozens of them by the time the Lycans realized the Vampires had turned against them. Lycans got away and fled to this area. They figured Vampires wouldn't chase them this far into the wilderness since there were almost no humans to feed from. Gargoyles were already here, due to that same reason. They'd come over here from Europe to escape attacks by both Vampires and humans. They also had problems from time to time with other Gargoyle clans attacking."

"Why would Gargoyles attack each other?"

"Power. Territory. The same reasons all races fight."

"Gargoyles really exist..."

"Not a lot of full-bloods remain in the local clan these days. Once there were maybe two dozen male Gargoyles. My father said they only had a few Gargoyle women." He paused. "Gargoyles birth mostly boys. It's a genetic tendency they have. Female Gargoyles are a rarity, probably one in twenty births."

"That's not good, unless they have nineteen husbands each."

He shook his head. "Gargoyles are territorial. They wouldn't share a woman. It meant they'd fight each other to the death to win the favor of a perspective mate. Then all of a sudden, there were a lot of single Lycan females, since most of the unmated males didn't survive the war."

"I think I see where this is heading."

Red nodded. "They each needed something from the other. Lycans were looking for sanctuary and a strong alliance to help them defend their women and children from Vampires if they tracked them to this area. Gargoyles needed women to breed them children."

"Poor Lycans. It's like out of the frying pan and right into the fire."

"Not quite." Red shook his head. "They weren't forced into anything by the Gargoyles. It was all voluntary. Unattached Gargoyle men were introduced to unmated Lycan women. If they were attracted to each other and both agreed, they'd mate. GarLycans were born of those unions."

"But you're partners still, right? Allies? Why don't you trust them?"

"We're good now but it was stressful for a long time. They resented that some of the Lycans were already pregnant or had given birth to children from the war. The VampLycans. Full Gargoyles look down on us half-breeds because of our Vampire blood, but we both still have full-blooded Vampires as a common enemy. Their prejudices have kept us on our toes."

"If they have kids with half Lycan and Gargoyle blood, doesn't that make their kids half-breeds too?"

"Yes."

"That's stupid."

"I agree…but Gargoyles have a superiority complex. They hate everything Vampire and have taught that hatred to their children. Gargoyles had their own war with that race in Europe that lasted for thousands of years. But one GarLycan has recently mated a half human with VampLycan blood. We're not sure how that's going to work out with the GarLycans. They still mostly refuse to breed with anyone from our clan. They don't want the Vampire bloodline to taint their precious Gargoyle heritage. They're starting to have the same problem as before though, so maybe they'll soften up on that rule. There are more men than women in their clan, but we no longer have any full-blood Lycan females for them to choose from."

She swallowed hard. "Can you back away now? Why am I even in this position?"

"I wasn't attempting to control your mind."

"Your eyes were glowing. I know that power."

"True. I'm a VampLycan, though."

"What does that mean?"

He lowered his gaze to her breasts. "They glow when I'm horny, too."

Oh shit. She swallowed hard, taking in that bit of information with an erratically beating heart. "You have a girlfriend. Put me down."

Annoyance flashed across his features. "She isn't my girlfriend."

"You admitted to only having sex with women who don't live in your town. I currently qualify as a resident. Thanks but no thanks. I'm not into casual sex. Put. Me. *Down*."

He didn't budge. "You're not a resident. You're a visitor."

"Red...? Back off." Fear spiked for a second. What if he didn't? What if he wasn't as honorable as she'd thought? She'd felt safe until he'd pinned her against the wall and did the glowing-eyes thing. "I don't want to get hurt again."

"I would never force you."

"I meant heartbreak. I don't do casual sex for a reason. My body and heart are a package deal. I can't put it any plainer than that. You have a woman out there. You're talking about living with her, and one day you'll meet your mate. I don't want to just warm your bed because the girlfriend isn't here or until you find someone better."

He frowned, studying her. "Is that how you see it?"

"I like keeping things real, and that's what it boils down to. There's a lot I don't know about your kind but that mate thing is pretty solid. I'd be dumped instantly if you found yours, right? Nature calling and all that. Thanks, but no. I'm old enough now to know better. I like my heart in my chest and not ripped out."

He scowled. "I wouldn't allow anyone to hurt you."

"I mean *emotionally* ripped out. But I'm glad to know you won't let your girlfriend shred me to death if she shows up here. She'd kick my ass."

His expression softened. "I like you, Emma."

"I like you, too. But that doesn't mean we can have sex." She was tempted though. She hadn't ever been attracted to anyone as much as she was to Red. It also made her aware she might fall in love with him if they grew intimate. "*Please* back off? I can't take having my heart broken again."

He slowly released her. She breathed easier when he put space between them by walking to the stove. She studied his broad back as he yanked open a cupboard to remove plates.

"This is going to be difficult."

She stayed where she was. "What is?"

"Wanting you and being this close."

"You said you had to get supplies. Maybe you should do that today. I'm sure I'll be safe here alone for a few hours."

"Yes. Fresh air would do me good. All I can smell is you."

"Like bloodlust and being hungry?"

He turned his head and stared at her. "I want to fuck you. Not eat you." His gaze lowered to the area between her thighs. "God." He swung his head back around. "I would totally eat you—but not like a Vamp feeds off women. I'd love to bury my face between your legs and put my mouth on you."

Heat bloomed in her body. He was talking about oral sex. She bet he'd be good at it, too. He had enough rough edges that she doubted he'd do anything half-assed. That warmth spread lower to her belly and a slight throbbing began at her clit.

"You really should get supplies today."

He faced the kitchen. "I'll do that right after we have breakfast."

"Good."

She watched him move, noticing those big arms, the way his muscles bunched and flexed, and she stared at his beefy ass encased in faded denim. It was safe to study him when he wasn't aware of it. She imagined what it would be like to rake her fingernails down his back, and an image of having him against her again flashed in her mind. The urge to touch him became almost overwhelming.

Red dished out food onto plates resting on the small counter and turned around. She jerked her attention to his face, staring into his eyes. His nostrils flared, drawing her gaze lower as he inhaled.

Then he moved fast enough to remind her of a Vamp, suddenly invading her space. He didn't touch her, but was so close, only a few inches separated them.

"*Fuck*." He growled.

His deep tone only made the warmth worse.

It surprised her when he took a step back and just dropped to his knees. He used his big hands to clasp her hips then lowered his head, staring intently at the vee of her pants.

He pressed his face there, and she gasped, not expecting that.

He buried his nose right where her clit was, rubbing it through the material. "You're so *hot*, baby. I can smell you…" He moved his head, continuing to torment her with that slight brush of his nose.

Emma closed her eyes. Desire rolled through her like never before. She had to lock her knees to keep from sliding to the floor. Red growled, creating vibrations. Emma moaned and blindly reached out, grabbing ahold of his shoulders.

Red moved his hands, sliding his fingers into the waist of her pants. He fisted the material and pulled hard. The zipper of her jeans broke under his strength. He jerked her pants down as he inched his face away.

Emma opened her eyes, staring down at him.

He reached up again, gripped her underwear, and slid them down in one rough tug. He hooked her pants where they'd been shoved down her thighs and tore both garments lower.

"Step out."

"Red…I…" She wanted him so bad it hurt. Was she going into heat? It had never happened before but she couldn't ignore the painful need to have him touch her.

His head snapped up and his eyes were golden again. She didn't look away this time, trusting that he wasn't going to take over her mind. He was just turned on, too. "This was bound to happen between us, Emma. Don't say no," he rasped. "Let me, baby."

She was forty years old. It had been ten years since she'd taken a chance on a man. "I don't want to get hurt."

"Don't you want to find out what's between us? I've felt drawn to you since the moment we met."

He'd appeared pretty irritated to have her thrust into his life, but staring into his beautiful golden eyes, she found herself nodding.

He shoved her pants lower and she lifted one leg, helping him take them off. Her panties were tangled with the jeans material now. He tugged them free and she raised the other leg, freeing it.

She expected them to move toward the bed but Red had other ideas. He just hooked one of her knees with his hand and lifted, placing it over his shoulder.

Emma gasped when he buried his face again.

Nothing was between them anymore. His hot mouth nestled in and he used his tongue against her clit. Emma slid her fingers into his hair. Moans tore from her as Red licked and sucked on the sensitive bundle of nerves. He growled, adding the vibrations again.

No one had ever touched her with that much enthusiasm. It was too intense, and Red didn't hold back. Emma bit her lip, attempting to muffle some of the sounds she made. Her belly clenched and she started to buck her hips, unable to hold still. Red grabbed her ass, his fingers digging into her skin to keep her in place.

"I can't take it!" she cried out. She fisted his hair, trying to pull him off.

He snarled and became rougher, his tongue moving faster. Emma threw back her head against the wall and closed her eyes again. Ecstasy tore through her and she forgot how to breathe. The one leg she stood on would have collapsed except Red kept her pinned against the wall with his body.

He jerked his mouth away as she rode the climax through.

Emma was aware of Red releasing her ass and sliding his palms upward. He suddenly shifted his shoulder, forcing her leg to drop. She fell forward, off balance. Red rose up, lifting her right off her feet. Once again, Emma found herself draped over his shoulder.

He strode to the bedroom area and dropped to his knees. The mattress cushioned their fall when he bent forward, gently dumping her onto the bed. She opened her eyes, staring up at him.

He reached down, unfastening his pants.

"You're so beautiful."

Emma loved his raspy voice and the way he lowered his gaze, taking her in. It made her feel desirable, and he sounded sincere. She arched her back and struggled with her shirt. She didn't want it in the way. It also helped distract her when Red shoved his pants down his hips. She didn't want to gawk.

She tugged the material over her head and twisted her arms, undoing her bra. She flung it out of the way. Red dropped down over her, using his arms to brace his upper body to prevent him from crushing her with his weight. He lowered until their chests were touching, staring deeply into her eyes.

"I'll be gentle."

It was a reminder to them both that she was mostly human. It also made her wonder how he usually had sex. It was probably not slow and easy. He was big and super strong. He'd proven that last part many times.

"Say yes."

It was more a demand than a request but Emma didn't mind. She wanted him. The damage was done and there was no going back. She didn't want to call a stop to it.

"Yes."

She spread her legs wider apart and lifted them, wrapping her thighs around his hips. Red shifted his position a little and she felt the broad tip of his cock nudge against her pussy. She stilled, holding her breath. He kept staring at her, not looking away. She liked that.

He slowly pressed against her, and she realized how wet she had become, her body more than prepared to accept Red. His cock felt big as he started to enter. She could feel her body stretching to accept the thickness of his girth. She bit her lip and grabbed hold of his shoulders.

His eyes narrowed and low growl emanated from him when he froze. "You're going to be the death of me yet, Emma."

It was a seriously bad idea to have sex with Red. Everything she'd said had been true. She wasn't the type to have casual sex. The last thing she needed was to fall for yet another man who would break her heart.

She raised her legs a little, gripping him tighter to urge him on.

Red sank in deeper—and it felt amazing. There was no pain or discomfort. She just ached for more, wanting all of him. He lowered his mouth but didn't go for her lips. He tilted his head slightly and she closed her eyes.

He kissed her neck. A shiver ran down her spine, the good kind, when she felt fangs lightly brush her skin. She'd never wanted a man to bite her before but Red was changing everything. She even twisted her head to give him better access.

She'd never felt as close to a person as she did at that moment. He was all around her, on top of her, pinning her under him. Their bodies were intimately joined. He froze again when she was pretty sure his cock was completely inside her. He was incredible hard. Another growl rumbled from him, and she liked the way his chest vibrated against hers...his lips too.

"Oh, fuck," he groaned.

"What?" She opened her eyes.

"You feel so *right*." He paused, then licked her skin. "*Taste* so right. Smell so damn good..."

She could relate. He smelled good too, and sex had never felt better. She slid one hand down his back, lightly raking her fingernails over his hot skin. His fangs gently nipped her throat in response. He didn't break skin but it felt incredible. Her entire body responded and she bucked under him, wanting him to move.

He wiggled his hips, easing away a little. It felt amazing but it made her ache. The desire for sex had never been stronger. It became a physical pain. "Please!" She wasn't sure exactly what she was asking for but hoped *he* would know. It was her first time in heat, if being around someone like him had caused this reaction.

"Do you want me to stop?" He sounded tormented.

"No! Not that."

"I don't want to hurt you."

"You won't. Please, Red. I want more..."

He drove back in, not as gently. Emma cried out as rapture jolted her entire body with surge of passion. Red snarled and tucked his head, nibbling kisses down the top of her shoulder where her neck ended. He spread his legs a little wider, pinning her tighter to the bed. Her nails dug into him, probably leaving marks.

Then he thrust fast and deep, pounding in and out of her.

Emma cried out and squeezed her eyes closed. She could only cling to Red. He fucked her too fast for her to attempt to meet his tempo. The world fell away. There was just Red and the pleasure pouring between them. Sweat slicked their bodies and her nipples rubbing against his chest just amplified the raw sensations swamping her senses.

It built until she couldn't think. Her body tensed, every muscle seeming to spasm. The climax struck and she cried out. Red tore his mouth away from her neck and snarled again, right against her ear.

It barely registered to Emma, too lost as her mind was blown.

Chapter Five

Red managed to keep enough weight off Emma to make certain she could breathe. Her ragged pants were a match to his own. He fought to regain some sanity. It was tough to do. He'd just come so hard inside her that his nuts ached. Small tremors racked his body as he shifted his head a little to unhook his fangs from the bedding he'd ravaged when he'd bitten into it, rather than her.

Sweat coated his body and probably hers. He always pulled out before he came, to avoid a woman carrying his scent for longer than a quick shower to wash him off her skin. It was a sobering realization to know he hadn't. His dick softened slightly but he was still snuggly nestled inside the warm confines of her pussy.

He didn't want to separate their bodies. He just remained still, keeping her exactly where he wanted her. Under him. Her arms were wound around his neck and her calves rested over his ass. Even the sides of her knees planted near his ribs, trapped between his torso and arms, seemed nice. She felt so damn right and had been extremely responsive to him.

This is not good. She's never been around another VampLycan. What if my hormones affected her and that's why she agreed to let me bed her?

Her body wouldn't have been tested by a human. They didn't have the right chemistry to tempt her Lycan side to appear. That had to be it—because otherwise they were both in deep shit if she was as drawn to him as he was to her.

He opened his eyes as he lifted his head a little, staring at the pale column of her exposed throat and the top of her shoulder. There were slight red marks from his mouth but no blood. It was tempting to bite. *Too damn tempting.* He tore his gaze off that area and studied her face.

Her eyes were closed and her skin rosy. Her lips looked so incredibly kissable, parted as she tried to catch her breath. That was another urge he fought. He couldn't pull back his fangs at that moment to save his life. He hadn't meant to sprout them at all. Emma brought out the animal inside of him.

He glanced at his upper arms, relieved that he hadn't grown a little more hair. That would *really* freak her out if he'd partially begun to shift while he'd fucked her. Small slips could happen if the sex was good enough.

Good enough? Fuck.

He couldn't even compare other women to Emma. He'd never totally lost control before, yet he did with her. *So much for gentle and slow.* He'd gone at her as if *he'd* been the one in heat. He dared to breathe through his nose, and the scent of her made him stifle a groan. His dick stiffened and engorged with blood. He wanted her again. She smelled like pure sex and heaven to him. Better than food to a starving man, or any than damn thing he'd ever scented.

Emma opened her eyes and he stared into them. He saw a spark of confusion, quickly followed by fear. He didn't blame her, if she was thinking or feeling anything close to what he was experiencing. He was a bit confused and scared too.

What if she was his mate? Life *couldn't* be that fucked up.

Red might be kin to his clan leader but his uncle had expectations. Uncle Velder had made it clear that he depended on Red to do what his sons hadn't.

Shit. This is so bad.

His uncle could ask him to leave with Emma if she was his mate. Other clans might not want them either if Vampires were after her. It would be putting their young at risk if they were attacked because of someone they didn't know, nor care about. He'd have to protect her on his own and live in the human world if that were the case. He wasn't sure he could keep her safe under those circumstances.

Emma caressed his shoulder and he quivered. It felt too good. He longed to have her stroke every part of him...

It was another sign of a possible mate, and he needed to put space between them. Otherwise he'd fuck her again until he did something stupid, like bite her. One drop of her blood could seal them together forever if he went nuts. He'd mate her if she was the one—and nothing would stop him. Not even the fact that he hadn't discussed it with her first. He'd just claim what was his and consequences be damned.

His dick throbbed, reminding him that he was inside her. He slowly withdrew, clenching his teeth because it felt so incredible that he never wanted to leave. It was with deep regret that he pulled out. He had to shift his hips a little so he wasn't lined up to enter her again. He wanted to do that more than taking his next breath.

"Red?"

Her whispered voice sounded puzzled, making him reconsider his actions. She might be going into heat. That meant *he* had triggered it.

Distance was needed between them before it was too late. But he didn't want to hurt her feelings or make things worse by just pulling away. That meant he had to explain what was going on.

He just hoped she'd understand.

"We need to stop."

"You're still hard. I felt you." Pink rushed to her cheeks. "I…we could do it again."

She was naïve in so many ways. It tore at his guts. He'd love to agree. She wanted him too. He almost lost his will to do the right thing.

It was one of the toughest things he'd ever done when he lifted, putting a little space between their chests. He couldn't resist glancing down. She had beautiful breasts, and he actually salivated, wanting to play with them with his mouth. She did taste so sweet. He could lick her all over.

He turned his head and closed his eyes, breathing through his mouth. It didn't help much. His heart raced and he fought with desire. It almost overpowered him. He wanted Emma too much.

"Fuck!"

He needed to put more space between them or he was going to lose his willpower. He shoved himself up and rolled toward the edge of the bed, tearing out of her hold. She wasn't strong enough to keep a tight grip on him. He got to his feet and took a few steps away. He stopped, feeling torn between wanting to get back in bed with her and running outdoors to find fresh air not saturated with her scent.

Her breathing changed. He was very aware of everything about her. He could even hear her erratic heartbeat. She shifted on his bed, the noise so slight, but he could still detect it. He took a few deep breaths through his mouth, forcing his mind to conquer the urges of his body.

"Red? What's wrong?"

He shook his head and turned. She had sat up and pulled the cover over her breasts and lap. It helped cool some of his desire. He could see she was baffled, and he was even pretty sure that slightly pained expression on her face meant he'd hurt her feelings. He understood.

"I wanted to bite you." He just blurted it out.

She eased her grip on the blanket and reached up, gently touching the spots where he'd used his fangs to hold her in place. The red marks were more vivid now, would probably leave a bruise. *A love bite without broken sink, thankfully.*

"It would have been okay."

Yeah, she is too naïve.

"You said VampLycans can bite during sex. I wouldn't have freaked out on you."

She was almost urging him to do it. He took a step closer to her, tempted. He fisted his hands at his sides and halted. "I need to shower." *And put space between us. Wash off your scent. Find my damn sanity. My control is slipping.*

Her gaze lowered to his dick. He knew what she saw. He was rock hard still, and probably would remain that way for as long as she stayed in his vicinity. She looked up at his face and frowned. It made his chest hurt when he saw the shine of unshed tears fill her eyes. She curled her knees up tight to her body under his blanket, grasping it with one hand, seeming to take a protective posture.

"Okay."

He'd hurt her, alright. It was the last thing he wanted. "You don't understand."

She turned her head away, staring at part of his bed. "Yes, I do."

"What do you think you understand?" His temper sparked just a little.

"Go take your shower. The food is getting cold."

She wouldn't look at him again and there was definite pain in her voice. He spun in the opposite direction and walked to where he kept his spare clothes, grabbing a loose pair of cotton running shorts. He put them on. They didn't hide the fact that he was still sporting a major boner but it made him feel a little more secure being so close to her, now that both of them were partially covered. He faced her again.

"Emma."

"What?" She fingered the fur on his bed.

"Goddamn it," he snarled.

That made her lift her head and stare into his eyes. The tears were still there and it ripped at his guts. She said nothing. He had plenty to say.

"I wanted to bite you."

"That's what you said."

"That would be bad."

"Because I'm too human. Got it."

"I didn't say that." He paused. It was true though. He'd have bitten her to find out for certain if she was his mate if she'd been from one of the clans. "I have accepted a blood oath to keep you safe. That means even from myself."

"You didn't plan to rip out my throat, did you?" She scowled.

"No."

"Then what are you trying to say?"

He didn't dare draw any closer. "I wanted to bite you because...I think it's possible you could be the one."

Her lips parted and her eyes widened.

"My mate. You smell too good and too tempting, Emma. Do you understand? What happened between us became too intense. It wasn't normal. I'm also pretty sure my pheromones are screwing up yours. I could send you into full-blown heat if I don't get away from you. You're reacting to me too strongly—as in *Lycan* response. Understand?"

She chewed on her bottom lip, studying him. She blinked a few times and her expression changed to what he guessed was anger. "Let's end this conversation now. You should go take that shower."

"I don't want you to be hurt."

"I'm not." She shoved the blanket away and stood.

His knees almost gave way beneath him when the sight of her bared breasts and every other inch of her was revealed. It made him want her all over again. His erection became painful as it strained against the material of the shorts, bent at an awkward angle. He reached down and adjusted.

Emma watched him do it and stalked closer. He would take her to the floor to fuck her if she touched him. All self-restraint would be gone.

But she passed him, keeping inches of space between them. He turned his head, watching her hips sway as she entered the living room area. She bent and he twisted fully, staring at her ass. He wanted to rush over there and shove down his shorts to get them out of his way. The image of turning her a little, pinning her over the arm of the couch and fucking her from behind, filled his head.

She yanked clothes out of her bag and straightened, dressing as he watched. He hated seeing her cover her body. He didn't protest though. Just held himself still, her every movement holding his rapt attention. She ignored him to enter the kitchen next. It was as if he no longer existed to her.

It pissed him off.

"Emma?"

She was ignoring him. She proceeded to eat while standing at the counter, her back to him. She had to have heard him. He knew it would be smart to go take that shower and cool his lust.

Instead, he took a few steps closer to her.

"Emma," he growled.

She raised one delicate hand over her shoulder. It was fisted. Her middle finger shot up and she held that pose for a few seconds before dropping it from his sight.

That was it. She was a spitfire, and she'd certainly got his blood boiling. He advanced, telling himself it was a bad idea. But it happened too fast for him to reason with himself.

He gripped her hips and spun her around, pinning her against the counter.

She gasped, and he *hated* the flash of fear he saw as he peered down at her. He'd never hurt her. He was aware of their size differences though, understanding why she might be wary. She was too damn short and small. A VampLycan female was more robust and sturdier.

He gentled his hold.

"Don't flip me off."

"Or you'll what? Hit me?" She raised her chin defiantly and her anger seemed to override her fear. "Bite me? Toss me out of your metal coffin buried in the ground? Go ahead. I *told* you we shouldn't have sex. You wouldn't listen." She reached up and pushed on his chest. "Let go of me. I'm too *human* to touch."

She was driving him insane already. "Do you *want* to be mated to me?"

Confusion clouded her eyes. She didn't answer him.

"That's what I think will happen if I taste your blood. I'd mate you, damn it! I wouldn't even ask. I nearly lost my mind while I was inside you." He leaned closer and bent his legs a little to put their faces closer together. "I'd bite you, and make you bite me. I'd fuck you for days, until we were starving and I had no choice but to leave to get more food. But I wouldn't want to do so until our bond had grown strong. I wouldn't be able to part from you even for a short time otherwise."

She looked stunned. He didn't blame her. She said nothing while he took a few ragged breaths. He calmed, barely.

"My uncle wants me to mate to a VampLycan on top of everything else. Both of his sons mated half-breeds with human blood. I told him I wouldn't let him down. I hate to break my word…but you're making me rethink that, Emma. Do you understand? *That's* how tempted I am to test a mating. Say the word and I'll bite you. Just know that if I react the way I think I will, your ass is going to be mated to me in the next ten minutes."

Her features softened and she stopped pushing against his chest. Her palms just rested there. He liked her touch too much. Hell, he wanted to pull her into his arms and kiss her. It would end with them back on his bed and his fangs buried in some part of her anatomy, along with his dick. He refrained.

"Getting out of that bed was the hardest thing I've ever done. Can you comprehend that? Don't make this worse than it already is by taking my actions wrong, Emma. You would be running from me if you knew how bad I want to rip off your clothes and fuck you again."

She glided her hands from his chest to his shoulders. He closed his eyes at the sparks of pleasure she gave him and made the mistake of inhaling through his nose. Her clothes did a poor job of hiding her scent. He groaned.

"Red?"

He opened his eyes and stared down at her. "What?" He wanted to wince at how gruff his voice came out.

"Go shower." Her anger appeared gone. "I thought you regretted having sex, or that you were just using me for a one-time deal. I get it now. I do. You didn't expect to react to me that way. I don't know you well enough to make that kind of commitment if you did bite me, and it turns out that you like my blood." She softened her tone. "We're okay. I'll warm the food for you while you wash."

React to her that way? Like her blood? That was putting it mildly. He wanted to snarl. She just didn't understand. It wasn't her fault, though. She'd been raised by a Vampire.

He let go of her hips with reluctance and inched away until her hands weren't touching him anymore. He spun, making a hasty retreat into the bathroom.

He closed the door and flipped on the light, stripping. Icy water pelted him when he twisted the knobs and it helped cool his overheated body and libido. He dumped shampoo into his hand and held it close to his nose, hoping it would help him forget her scent long enough to get total control of his mind and body.

His life had undergone a drastic change in the space of a day. Yesterday, he'd been contemplating allowing a woman to move into his house to ease his loneliness. His biggest worries had been how he'd handle sharing a bed with someone else every night and whether they could get along without wearing on each other's nerves.

Then Emma arrived…and now he had to wonder how long he'd last before he tasted her blood. He wanted her to share his bed every single day and night. He didn't give a damn *how* they got along. He just wanted her close to him.

"Fuck," he growled.

Her grandfather was going to be a problem, too. Vampires were territorial. She'd been living with him since the age of four. Malachi would consider Emma part of his nest, and they had that mental bond she'd told him about. It made him feel jealous and irrational. Her grandfather wouldn't want to let her go, when and if he showed up in Howl to collect her.

It might mean they'd have to fight to the death.

Guilt immediately struck over the brief hope that the Vampires had killed Malachi. She'd never leave if her grandfather didn't show up to take her away. Red could keep her. It would break Emma's heart though, and he didn't want her to suffer grief.

He closed his eyes and fisted the soap, feeling it ooze through his fingers. This wasn't going to turn out well, no matter how things went down. She'd never forgive him if he ashed her grandfather, and he *would* if it turned out she was his mate. *Nobody* would ever take her from him.

He'd kill anyone who tried, even if it were the Vampire who'd raised her.

Emma only started eating again when she heard water come on in the bathroom. Her hand slightly shook.

Red had made everything very clear. She'd thought he was an asshole when he'd rolled off her right after they'd had sex. She'd felt used and stupid for allowing him to take her to bed. It hurt, and then it had made her furious.

But he wanted to bite her. Everything he'd said about a mate replayed in her head. She also understood the promise he'd made to his clan leader to mate a VampLycan. Once again, being mostly human had become a negative against her.

She stared at the door that led to the stairwell out of the den. She should grab her bag and take off while Red showered. It would be doing them both a favor.

The memory of the walk through the woods, being carried over his shoulder, stopped her from following through. She had to be deep in VampLycan territory. It would be like having an open wound and taking a stroll at midnight through a street with a Vampire nest in the vicinity. They'd sniff her out and she'd be surrounded before she could make it a mile.

Her grandfather would come for her as soon as it was safe. That could be days or even weeks. He'd want to make certain he didn't lead the Vampires to her. She knew the drill. The last time they'd been found, they'd spent a few weeks touring Canada before boarding a flight to New York. From there, they'd gone west. They'd changed identities half a dozen times just to be certain no one could track them. They would have remained safe in their house, but some Vamps had moved into the area.

One call to the Vampire Council and her world had come crashing down.

She lost her appetite and sat on the couch, curling up into a ball. What if her grandpa hadn't escaped? Eduardo had already defied his master once. Did a jerk like that really care about following laws? He was crazy, and probably just using the council as a means to gain help in finding them. It was possible he was ready to end his own life but determined to take his master out with him.

Her grandpa might never show up for her.

It was a terrifying concept. She'd be alone in the world. She smelled and looked human. She'd have to constantly live on the move every few years to avoid them growing suspicious that she wasn't one of them when she didn't age the way she should. The Vampires would kill her outright if they ever guessed her mother had been a VampLycan. Lycan packs would fear and hate her too. The VampLycans probably wouldn't accept her because she was too human to shift. GarLycans would hate her just because her grandfather was a Vampire and she carried some of his blood in her veins.

Screwed any way I look at it.

Overwhelming sadness choked her. She and her grandfather had always been outcasts but at least they'd had each other to depend on. *He has to be alive. He's coming for me.* She needed to believe that.

The water cut off in the bathroom and she wiped away the tears. Red had finished with his shower.

Red was another example of how her heritage would never allow her to have any kind of normal life. She hadn't missed the look in his eyes when he'd told her about the promise he'd made. He might have said he'd risk breaking his word, but he seemed like an honorable man. That would hurt someone like him. He'd grow to resent her if she allowed him to bite her and take her for his mate. A lifetime with a bitter partner sounded like hell on Earth.

She just had the worst luck when it came to men…only this one was too noble instead of a douchebag. It looked as if she were destined to become that old maid she'd told him she wasn't.

Even if she was willing to risk Red resenting her, and decided to let him bite, being his mate would be bad for another reason. Her grandfather had talked about the days when he'd lived in Alaska. He'd had a Lycan companion then, someone to drink blood from. Her grandmother had died though. She doubted the clan members would offer up their wrists to keep him fed. Grandpa wouldn't accept her blood on a regular basis, and she doubted Red would allow her to offer if she were his mate. That meant she'd have to stay with Red while her grandfather had to leave.

She was all he had. He'd be alone. The thought wrenched at her heart.

The bathroom door opened and she kept her gaze averted. He'd leave for a few hours to get supplies, and dangerous or no, she needed to come up with an alternative plan while he was gone. It was completely out of the question to remain with Red inside his den. Her body ached for him. The constant awareness of her swollen clit and her oversensitive nipples wasn't exactly comfortable. It would fade away once she wasn't near the testy VampLycan anymore. He'd caused it, and getting away from him would end it.

She glanced up when he left the bedroom. He entered the kitchen wearing faded jeans, a blue long-sleeve shirt, and a pair of black tennis shoes. He picked up the plate of corned-beef hash she'd forgotten to reheat. He didn't say a word, just ate. He rinsed his empty plate in the small sink.

"I'll be gone three hours tops."

"Okay."

He turned to face her, and she made the mistake of looking at him again.

Red frowned and drew closer. "Are you okay?"

"Yes." She lowered her chin, studying her hands in her lap.

"Look at me."

She did. He crossed the room and crouched, staring deeply into her eyes.

"You've been crying." His voice softened. "I didn't mean to hurt your feelings." Then he sniffed at her—and his eyes began to glow. "You *are* going into heat. I was hoping my pheromones just temporarily affected your sex drive."

"Your what?" He'd mentioned something about that before but she hadn't really let it click.

"Dominant Lycan men can give off a scent that attracts sexual interest from women when we're really turned on. It's not something one controls. It's like getting a hard-on, only we get a scent to go with it. You've never smelled it before, and it might be hitting you stronger than it should under normal circumstances. You wouldn't have built up a tolerance. The horniness you felt should have faded when I gave you some space. Are you in pain?"

"I'm fine. It's a little uncomfortable. I'll take a shower while you're gone. Maybe that will help."

"Or maybe it won't." He reached out and touched her leg.

She jerked away. "Go, Red. I'll be fine."

"Not if you go into heat and stay that way. It will turn into a form of torture." He touched her forehead. She twisted away to break the connection.

"You're running a slight fever." His eyes grew brighter, golden.

"The shower will help cool me down."

"This is serious, Emma."

"Will it kill me?"

"No."

"Then *go*."

"I can't leave you this way."

"You already did when you rolled away from me earlier, Red. You said it yourself. You wanted to bite me, and we can't allow that to happen." She gripped the edge of the couch and used it to help her stand, avoiding brushing against him.

She made it a few feet when his next words stopped her dead in her tracks.

"You've had a little time to think, Emma. Do you want to risk being my mate? I'll have you in my bed in three seconds flat if you do."

It stunned her. She turned around, gawking at him.

He rose to his full height. "I'm no coward. I've always wanted to find my mate. We could test it out."

"You said you made a promise. I don't want you to break it."

Pain clouded his eyes, extinguishing the vivacious light inside them. "I also said I would if you're my mate."

"But you don't seem happy about that. Is it because I'm so human?"

"No. It's the promise I made to my uncle. I hate to break my word, but a true mate bond is more important—bottom line. He wanted me to mate a VampLycan."

"What's the difference?"

He hesitated. "Between what some call a true mate bonding and settling with someone as a mate?"

She nodded.

"The depth of the emotions are far deeper if it comes naturally. We form mental bonds stronger with true mates. Settling is more of a commitment to be together, rather than a deep-seated need to be with that person until death."

"That sounds like a huge difference, Red."

"It is." He regarded her with an intense stare.

"What about you? Did you ever imagine you might be drawn to someone like me?"

"No."

"You always dreamed of mating a strong VampLycan, didn't you?"

He didn't answer. His grim expression said it all.

She turned away. "Go get supplies. I'll be fine."

"Damn it, Emma!"

"Your mother doesn't like you to cuss in front of women, remember? Don't change on my account." She entered the tiny bathroom and closed the door.

Hot tears filled her eyes and she let them fall as she undressed. It was like playing Twister with a toilet and sink in the way. She just shoved her discarded clothing in the sink and turned on the water. It was still warm at least, from when Red had used it before her. She stood under the spray with her eyes closed.

Chapter Six

Red was furious. Emma was the only thing he could think about as he returned to Howl. She was stubborn and infuriating, preferring to suffer being in heat rather than allow him to take her back to bed. Sure, he had freaked out at first when he'd realized what might be happening, but the time spent cooling off in the shower had helped him get things in perspective. He was willing to risk tasting her blood to learn the truth.

The first person he saw in town made him wince. Uncle Velder stepped into his path and crossed his arms over his chest.

"Is there something you wish to explain to me, nephew?"

"I take it you heard about me carrying a woman into the woods."

"A human. Since when have I allowed that to happen? They aren't playthings for you to bring into our territory if you want to have sex with one."

"She's mixed blood."

"No other clan leader asked my permission for her to enter our territory. I went to your home last night but you weren't there. I assume she's inside your den?"

"Yes."

"I'll give you two minutes to explain. Start now."

"Emma's not from another clan. She's the granddaughter of Malachi. My father owed him a blood oath and she came here seeking protection. I was honoring his word by giving her what she needed."

"Malachi?" Velder appeared stunned. "The Vampire?"

"You probably knew him, since he was around when the clans first formed." He hadn't thought of that until now.

"Of course. You said she's his granddaughter? That means she's VampLycan. Witnesses said they detected only a human scent. How is that possible?"

"Her mother was a VampLycan. Her father wasn't. She takes after him."

"Why is she here, exactly?"

This was the part he hated to admit. "Emma and Malachi are being hunted by his nest, who also recruited other Vampires to help track them down. As I said, Malachi sent her to my father for protection."

"Why?"

"He and Dad were friends."

"I know that part. Why is the nest hunting them?"

Emma's words flashed in his mind but he wasn't about to say Eduardo was "butt hurt" to his uncle. He wouldn't see the humor in that. "It seems Malachi formed a small nest, but he kept his VampLycan daughter, Kallie, and a few others in a nearby town under his protection." He paused. "Emma said a few VampLycans left Alaska with him. Is that true?"

Velder nodded. "Malachi had five children with his mate. Kallie was the only one who showed strong Lycan traits. The other four children, well...let's just say we didn't see them beyond sunup, after they'd hit puberty. Some Lycans donated blood to feed them but Malachi decided to leave when the Lycans did. We all worried about the children who showed strong Vampire traits. They didn't exactly want to fit in or play nice with other clan members. I'll guessing maybe that's the nest he formed. Three other VampLycans, aside from Kallie, went with that group. They refused to be parted from their mothers."

"Emma didn't mention having any uncles or aunts. I don't know what happened to them but they aren't with Malachi. Emma said her grandfather was her only family left. Malachi created one Vamp then took in strays to create his nest. I think they decided to attack the VampLycans, and then turned on Malachi. They killed Emma's mother but her grandfather rescued her. They've been living on the run ever since. The nest caught up to them a few days ago, and Malachi sent her here because his old nest involved the Vampire Council. She's mostly human. She'd be slaughtered in a fight against them."

Uncle Velder blew out a frustrated breath. "You didn't see fit to come to me right away with this?"

"I don't really believe they'll track her to us, and they'd be pretty stupid to come in here after her. It would be suicidal."

"That wasn't your decision to make."

Red's spine stiffened. "Fine. I'll take her and leave. I honor the Redwolf promises. My father owed Malachi a debt."

"I didn't say you had to leave."

Uncle Velder would allow Emma to stay. It made Red relax slightly…but he'd still broken the rules. "Thank you. I planned to talk to you today, and I know I'll face punishment for not telling you what was happening right away. I only ask that you wait until the danger is past if it's harsh enough to put me out of commission for a few days. I need to be able to fight if the situation arises."

"Make up your mind," his uncle muttered. "Either there is no threat, or you need to be strong to fight."

"I don't believe Vampires will show up here, but I'd rather be paranoid than unprepared."

"Understood." Uncle Velder dropped his arms to his sides and shifted his stance, taking on a more relaxed posture. He sighed. "Shit. We heard the Vampire Council sent a team after a Vampire associated with the original war. It must have been Malachi. But I wonder…why him? I'm going to have to make some calls. How's Malachi going to contact her when it's safe for her to leave? Does she have a phone number for him?"

"I believe he'll show up here to collect her when it's safe." He tensed, waiting for his clan leader to explode. No one wanted a Vampire just strolling into town.

"I'll let the others know to expect him."

The calm response surprised Red. "To prepare to attack him?"

"No. To let them know of his pending arrival. Malachi is no enemy of ours, Red. The younger ones like yourself wouldn't be aware of that, but the oldest generation remembers him well. He helped build this community and lived here with us for nearly two decades. He only left because he began to distrust his children's bloodlust. He put the clan's safety first."

"But he sent Emma here with the Vampire Council hunting for them both. Why would he do that?"

Uncle Velder sighed again. "He wouldn't—unless he believed they'd never follow her here, or assumed their fear of us would keep them away."

"Do *you* think that's why he sent her, instead of having her go to his other children?"

"He wouldn't trust them with his granddaughter's safety. They'd probably kill her themselves or hand her over to the nest who wants her. They became quite ruthless at puberty, and they definitely resented Kallie for being able to withstand the sun. I can't see them protecting her child. I'm sorry to hear of Kallie's loss. She was a sweet girl. Her siblings were not."

His uncle paused. "Extend Emma my condolences over her mother, and tell her the clan will help keep her safe until her grandfather arrives. Malachi will be welcomed here. Her mother was considered a member of our clan. That extends to Emma. There will be no punishment for you…but next time, inform me of a situation such as this. Consider it the only warning you'll get on the matter."

Red never saw *that* coming. He assumed Uncle Velder would snarl and perhaps do a lot of yelling after he'd explained the situation.

Instead, Velder considered Emma clan.

"May I ask something?"

"What?"

Red wasn't sure how to best broach the subject.

His uncle glowered. "I'm already angry with you for not coming to me right away. What else are you withholding? Spit it out."

"I think Emma might be my mate. Is it going to be an issue if she is?"

Now his uncle snarled.

Red clenched his teeth and kept his claws from sliding out. The urge to defend Emma was strong enough that he felt insulted for her. "Your sons mated Dusti and Bat. Is it okay for them but not me?"

"I'm just frustrated," his uncle admitted with a grimace. "It seems all the men in this family except myself have opted to seek out weak mates."

Red still fought the urge to hit his uncle. It would be a big mistake. To strike a clan leader, family or not, would be considered a challenge to his authority. A fight to the death would ensue.

"You know as well as I do that it's not a matter of seeking. And I wouldn't consider Emma weak. She just can't shift, Uncle Velder."

"I'm aware it's a big chunk of natural attraction. You must like this woman a hell of a lot. Why couldn't you fall for Cavasia? I know you two were considering trying to form a bond. She would have given you strong babies, and her clan leader already called to discuss her being accepted into ours. I would have agreed. "

"Cavasia doesn't make me feel the way Emma does. Is it going to be a problem or not?"

"I'll accept it if she *is* your mate...but you'd better hope your children take after *you*. I fear for our future if our next generation isn't strong enough to hold this clan together."

"Did you say that to Drantos and Kraven?" The answer would gauge how angry he became.

"I did."

"How did they respond?"

Uncle Velder suddenly grinned. "You probably want to punch me, too."

It was best not to answer that. "Are we done? I want to get back to my den."

"Yes. I want to hear from you every few days. Hunt for a cell signal and check in. I also wanted to warn you that Cavasia has heard about your visitor. She spoke to a few family members in our clan, trying to get information. You might want to address that before it becomes an issue. Emma is part of this clan and under our protection. Including from an angry woman who believed you were in negotiations with her to share a home."

"I'll take care of it."

"See that you do." His uncle walked away.

Red entered Peva's shop. The woman arched an eyebrow and hung up the phone to end the conversation to whomever she spoke to. "You've caused quite a stir, and you owe me. I didn't repeat anything I overheard between you and that human'ish person."

"Thank you. Her name is Emma."

"And why do you think I'd want to know that?"

"Because I consider you family. And I care about her."

Peva's surprise showed on her features. "Not another one. Seriously? What is it with you and your cousins?"

"I don't know what you mean."

Her eyes narrowed with suspicion. "I think you do. I heard your tone when you said you care about her. You're nailing her, aren't you? Did you take a little blood? Is she your mate?"

"I don't know."

"Ah-ha!" She pointed at him. "Which means you suspect she might be. I swear, you and your cousins have a craving for humans. I get it, though."

He scowled. "What's that supposed to mean?"

"You've been chased by about every woman in four clans. They're aggressive and pushy as hell. Humans aren't. It's probably a nice change of pace." She suddenly clutched her hands together over her chest and batted her eyelashes. "Save me, big VampLycan man! You're so strong and can fuck me like an animal." She burst into laughter. "The ego trip must be staggering."

"Shut up, brat." He was amused by her antics and needed the lighthearted moment after dealing with his uncle. "She isn't like that."

"I saw that stunt you pulled." She lowered her arms and gripped the counter between them, leaning forward. "Tossing her over your shoulder…and she let you carry her out of here. One of ours wouldn't have allowed you to do that. You'd have had a fight on your hands for treating them as if they couldn't walk."

"She gave me a little hell over it." He smiled. "She didn't look sturdy enough to make the hike to my den. I just wanted to get there fast."

Peva's features softened. "Admit it. It's nice to have a woman interested in *you* instead of your status with the clan."

"A bit."

"Is she totally clueless about us?"

"No, but I've had to fill her in on a few things."

"Do tell."

He hesitated. Peva was like a sister to him. He'd been very close to her older brother and had tried to fill in as her family after his death. His cousins had done the same. "She thought I was trying to control her mind when my eyes showed my emotions."

"When you got all hot and bothered." She glanced up and down his body. "I'm surprised she didn't scream. You probably scared her because of your size, and with the fact you're not being human. Has she figured out you're just a big pussy cat with claws yet?"

"I resent that."

She laughed. "Puppy dog then, with fangs. Better?"

"Much."

"Why are you here instead of home impressing her?"

"You *could* say her name."

She rolled her eyes. "Okay. Why aren't you with Emma? Don't tell me you need pointers on how to seduce a woman. I'm sure humans aren't that much different from our kind. Just avoid going all feral on her ass. The hair sprouting and snarling would probably be too much for her to handle."

"I wasn't stocked up properly at my den. I need supplies."

"Say no more." She turned away, going into the back.

Red reached over and picked up her store phone, dialing the number he knew by heart. He dreaded the call but it would take Peva some time to bag up what he'd need.

"Yes?" The familiar voice answered on the second ring.

"Hello," he got out. A lump formed in his throat. He hated to end their friendship but he was pretty certain the conversation would go that way.

"Red." She paused. "Is it true?"

"That would depend on what you've heard, Cavasia."

"You and a human are sharing your den?"

"She needed my help."

"Does this change things between us?"

"It does."

"I see." She paused. "I just wanted to know. Thank you for calling."

"You're welcome. I'm sorry about this."

"It's fine, Red. I don't love you. We had fun and I enjoyed our time together. I just wish you'd told me before I had to hear it from someone else. That was rude."

"It was unexpected. I only met her yesterday."

"You know my number when you grow bored of a human. I might still be lonely, but there's someone I've been curious about for a while. I think I'll approach him."

"I wish you the best."

"Thank you." She ended the call.

He hung up. Peva strolled out of the back with two bags. She placed them on the counter. "I'll bill your account. I put in some chocolate. Humans love that crap."

"Who doesn't?"

"Me. It's too sweet." She reached inside the left bag and grinned. "And these." She showed him the large box of condoms. "Humans can get pregnant. Try to avoid that until you're sure she's your mate. That would be awkward if she's not."

"That's not funny." He grabbed the box from her and laid them on the counter. "Thank you, but they aren't needed."

"You want to get her pregnant or is it that time of the month? Does she need pads?"

"No. She's on something to prevent that from happening."

"She can still get pregnant. You know that, right? It's almost that time of year and who knows how long she'll be here. You go into heat and it can void human birth control." She picked up the condoms and put them back inside the bag. "Better to be prepared and safe. Keep them."

"It's not that time for me."

"It could be if she's your mate. It happens. Your body goes all haywire and bam. You're suddenly in heat. Especially if you're insecure about whether she'll agree to accept you. You've got too much Lycan in you, Red. It will bite you in the ass. You know how tricky instincts and hormones can be. That part of you will make certain it can claim her any way it can, including planting a little Red baby in her belly."

"Thanks, Mom. I remember the talk about sex and our nature."

"You'd better clue your little human'ish in on it."

"Use her name and stop calling her that."

Peva grinned and leaned toward him until she stopped inches from his face. "Emma is your mate, you dumbass. So damn protective, and demanding I acknowledge her? Sure signs. Go." She pulled back. "I accepted the others. She'd better not fuck up by refusing to mate you. Little sis is also protective. I hate when you guys get hurt."

He lifted the bags in his arms. "I'll see you soon. Tell your mate I said hello and he still has my sympathy. You're such a brat."

The sound of her laugher followed him outside. He hurried his pace. He wanted to get back to Emma, worried that she really was going into heat. No amount of cold water would help with the fever if that were the case—but he could.

*****

Emma felt as if she wanted to die. She groaned, rolling over to lie on her stomach. She couldn't get comfortable on Red's bed no matter what position she tried. Her muscles ached and she was running a fever. She'd probably caught some nasty flu bug while traveling. Planes and buses were notorious for that. She rarely got sick but when she did, it was always bad.

She softly cursed aloud, knowing that was bullshit.

As much as she wished otherwise…she'd gone into heat.

No cold or flu had ever made her feel as horrible as she did at that moment. Red's pheromones had done a number on her body. She just hoped it didn't last long, since she had no clue how to make it stop. Her grandfather wasn't there to share a little of his blood to cure her. She wasn't even sure if that would work.

Stomach cramps had her groaning and rolling again, curling into a ball on her side. She fisted the soft blankets. Maybe Red had the ability to end her heat by donating some blood. She didn't know if it would be rude or considered taboo to ask him to help that way.

She kept the heavy blankets off to avoid sweating. Red's den was normally chilly, so she knew it was her body making it seem as if she'd suddenly been shoved into a sauna. Forty years, and *now* she'd gone into some kind of Lycan heat cycle. She'd never been around Werewolves. It must have been a dormant trait until Red hit her with his pheromones.

"And they put *humans* down, while Lycans have all this funky shit going on," she muttered. "This is so messed up."

Sudden noise alerted her that Red had returned. She didn't call out to him, but she didn't need to. His loud snarl let her know he was already aware of her distress.

"Hang on, Emma," he called out, his tone harsh. "Let me put this stuff in the fridge. I'm coming."

She tried to just breathe, focusing on pushing air in and out of her lungs. It helped with the pain a little. Red slammed things around in the kitchen. It seemed to take forever but it was probably only two minutes before he came to her.

"Damn," he growled. "I'm here."

She turned her head and forced her eyes open. Red tore at his shirt, removing it. His eyes were glowing golden, and she almost hoped he would take control of her mind to put her into a deep sleep.

"You're in full-blown heat."

"I was hoping it was the flu but I knew that was wishful thinking." She stifled a whimper. Her body felt as if it was being cooked from the inside out. "It's no longer a mystery why they call it heat. I'm burning up."

He bent, tearing off his shoes to get his pants off. "I know it's hell."

He straightened and stripped completely nude. She glimpsed how hard his cock was for a split second before he crawled onto the bed with her. He paused inches away, his gaze locked with hers when she looked at his face.

"Roll onto your back for me."

"I can't." She didn't want to move. It was agony. The fetal position on her side helped but not by much. It was the most comfortable one out of all the positions she'd tried.

Red nodded and eased closer, until he curled around her back. His big, firm body pressed tight against her skin made her feel less alone, and helped her focus more on him than the pain. He caressed her hip and lifted his head until his cheek brushed hers.

"I shouldn't have left you."

"We needed food."

"You needed me more."

"Just knock me out."

"The pain won't allow you to sleep. I'm going to get you through this." He slid his hand over the curve of her ass and lower, until his fingers brushed against the slit of her pussy. She knew she was soaking wet. "Trust me."

She didn't have a choice. "Can you give me blood to fix this?" It couldn't hurt to ask.

"There's only one way to make the heat better."

She cried out when he suddenly slid a thick finger into the channel of her pussy without warning.

It was pleasure and pain at the same time. Her senses were too confused to tell her if she should be alarmed. Red slowly moved his finger in and out of her...and she realized it wasn't pain after all. The pleasure was just super intense and sharp.

Red growled low next to her ear. "A little better?"

She released the blanket and frantically reached back, needing to touch him. His arm was in the way of her being able to grip his hip. She lifted her arm and found the back of his head, fisting his hair at the base of his neck.

"Can you spread your legs a little for me?"

She managed to part her knees a few inches and Red adjusted his body, sliding his down a little. He removed his finger from inside her entirely. Emma opened her mouth to protest but then something thicker and bigger pressed against the entrance of her pussy—and she cried out as Red's cock slid home deep.

He hissed. "*Fuck*."

That's exactly what they were about to do. He started to move inside her, and he gripped her hip again, holding her in place as he thrust in and out. Emma squeezed her eyes closed and moaned.

"Release my hair."

She was probably hurting him, so she let go. Red's hand slid from her hip, across her stomach, and he wiggled his fingers under her other hip. She gasped when he rolled them, not expecting him to lay flat and take her with him. She was sprawled over his body, on her back. Gravity forced her legs to fall to either side of his, and then he rolled again, pinning her on her stomach beneath him. He used one of his knees to push her legs farther apart. He braced his arms next to her shoulders. She could breathe easier when he lifted his chest off her back.

"Tell me if I'm too rough."

He started to thrust again, deep and fast. He hammered her with his cock, the sensations pure heaven. She clawed at the bed and cried out as the climax tore through her.

Red snarled but didn't slow his pace. He rode her even faster, his hips pounding against her ass. Emma wondered if she'd die from how much she was coming. Her heart felt as if it were about to burst and the top of her head seemed in danger of exploding.

Red growled loudly and froze on top of her. His dick seemed to have a pulse, throbbing against her oversensitive vaginal walls. He jerked, his entire body shaking over hers. Warmth spread, and she knew he was coming too.

He groaned…and started to fuck her again, slowly. The pace changing from frantic to tender.

He shifted his arms until he pinned her body tighter under him, his forearms resting on the bed. He also nuzzled her hair away from her shoulder and pressed a closed mouth kiss on her skin.

"I've got you, Emma." He kept moving inside her, fucking her with deep, leisurely strokes of his stiff cock. "I'm right here."

Sweat slickened her body. A lot of the burning sensation had faded, almost as if her fever had broken. The pain was gone, only to be replaced by an endless ache and the need for him to keep moving inside her. It felt amazing.

"Don't stop," she whispered, her voice a little hoarse from all the noises she'd made. She was afraid he'd roll away again and leave her on the bed alone.

"I won't." He opened his mouth, planting little licks and wet kisses along the top of her shoulder and the side of her neck. "I'm going to get you through this. Nothing could make me leave you."

It was nice to hear. She believed him. It even brought tears to her eyes that she blinked back, grateful he couldn't see them with her eyes closed and her face mostly buried against the bedding. He was taking care of her when he didn't have to.

She did feel a moment of panic that perhaps he'd lied, when he pulled out of her completely. She felt the loss immediately, the sensation of being empty a painful one. He lifted off her next.

She opened her eyes and twisted her head, staring at him. He got on his knees next to her and grabbed some of the pillows at the top of the bed. A frown twisted his lips when he looked at her.

"I'm not stopping. I'm just going to make this more comfortable for you. Get on your hands and knees."

He was a Lycan. The humor of the moment struck her. "You want to do it doggy style?"

His frown curved into a smile. "Not quite. You're exhausted from the pain. Trust me, Emma. This is going to feel good."

She managed to get on her hands and knees and Red started shoving pillows under her. She glanced at them, then looked back at him. She arched one eyebrow in question.

He chuckled. "I'm afraid I'm going to crush you with my weight." He pushed more pillows under her belly. "Close your legs."

"Okay." She put her knees together and watched as Red threw one of his legs over hers, positioning himself behind her. He gripped her hip with one hand and grabbed his dick with the other.

"Your arms are going to give way at some point. The pillows will keep your ass up." Humor glinted in his eyes. "Heat can last for days." He lowered his chin, staring at her. "Ready? I know *I'm* up for it."

She had to lift a little to see his erection. He remained hard. He moved in a little closer as he lined up with her pussy, pressing in. She moaned, and lost interest in watching as he entered her.

He gripped her other hip, holding her while he started to move. "Relax and enjoy this."

The pillows supported her lower half enough that she could do exactly as he'd instructed. She closed her eyes and just reveled in the feel of Red moving inside her. The climax was slower to build, matching the pace he set. When it struck, she cried out his name.

He paused for a few moments, letting her recover. Then he started moving inside her again. Emma clawed at the bedding. Red was going to kill her...but what a way to go.

Chapter Seven

Emma stood under the warm water in the shower and yawned. Every muscle in her body ached. It reminded her of the last time her grandfather had put her through self-defense training. Fighting against a four-hundred-plus-year-old Vamp had left her bruised and battered, despite him taking it easy on her.

She glanced down. There were no bruises on her that she could see but Red had definitely worked her over. Sex was way more enjoyable than getting beaten up.

She wasn't sure how long they'd been in bed together. It was a blur of pleasure and sleep, then repeat. The heat had faded though. She didn't feel feverish. All the aches she had now were from too much sex, not a need for it.

One thing was very clear though. She was falling for Red.

He'd been so tender and loving. She'd never forget the way he'd woken her with kisses and caresses. He'd put his mouth on every inch of her while they'd been in bed together. Even though he was in the other room, she could still almost hear his raspy voice telling her how beautiful he thought she was.

The things they'd done in that bed had been beyond intimate. She'd never experienced anything like it before and knew no one else would ever compare to him. The only regret she had was that he'd kept her from touching or putting her mouth on him. He'd been the one in control, pleasuring her. He'd told her it was because he still wanted to bite her, and it made it easier to resist the urge if she wasn't stroking his body with her hands.

She rinsed out the conditioner and knew she'd have to face Red. She turned off the water and used a towel to dry off the best she could. He wasn't in the bedroom area when she came out, but the bed had been stripped. She stared at the mattress as memories lingered of the hours they'd spent there.

"Come eat." Red's voice came from the kitchen.

She noticed the smell then. It made her smile. He seemed to really enjoy his steaks.

She didn't have clothes, so she stole one of his shirts from a drawer and put it on. It was big on her, more like a nightshirt. She threw the wet towel in the bathroom and joined him in the kitchen.

His hair remained wet from his own shower, which he'd taken before she'd climbed out of bed. He wore just a pair of low-hipped boxers. They were blue, a compliment to his tanned, muscled body. Desire shot through her, seeing how sexy he looked.

Her gaze lifted when he turned to face her. He grinned.

"Don't give me that look. I'm washing our bedding. I don't have spare sheets here."

"I didn't know you had a washing machine hidden." She glanced around the den.

"I don't. It's called a river, and a rock placed on top of them to keep them from floating away. I scrubbed them with soap first. I'm letting the sheets soak for a bit. Then I'll hang them to dry and air out."

"Wow. That's old school."

"I have a washing machine and dryer at the cabin. It's more modern than our den."

Our. She wasn't sure how to take that. Did he mean her? Or should she ask who else owned this den.

He placed a steak on a plate that already held a microwaved baked potato. He'd slit it open and placed butter inside.

He jerked his head toward the small table. "Go sit."

"Thank you, but I can carry my own food. You don't have to wait on me. I'm already not used to anyone cooking for me."

"That's right. Your grandfather doesn't eat food."

"Some Vampires do, if they're newer or never gave up food for blood only. He didn't know he had a choice after he was turned. He's had to eat meals a few times, but it's not pretty. It gives him horrible stomach cramps and he pukes everything up about an hour later. It's the only way to get it out of him."

Red's eyebrows arched.

"His digestive tract doesn't work the way it did when he was human, after all the years of not eating food. He can't pee or go number two," she explained.

"Why would he even bother to eat food then?"

"To fool humans."

"But why care that much? He could just wipe their memories if they get suspicious of his nature."

She hesitated, taking the plate and carrying it to the table. Red had set out silverware and extra butter. He'd even placed two sodas down so they each had a drink. He followed her to the table with his own plate.

"Is it a secret?"

She held his gaze. "Remember that guy I said I dated? The cheater? He wanted to meet my so-called 'brother' while we were together." She shrugged. "He insisted on us all having dinner together. I couldn't exactly tell him the truth. It's not something you just drop on someone. 'Oh, by the way, that's actually my grandpa, and don't bleed around him unless you want to risk him possibly biting you because he's a Vamp.'" She smiled to soften the sarcastic words. "Grandpa had dinner with us at a restaurant to avoid suspicion of anything being off in our family."

Red gripped his knife. "I see."

"There were a few other times. I told you I was in band during high school. Grandpa would go to the night events to see us perform. Sometimes, afterward, all us kids would go out for pizza. There were only so many times he could claim to have already eaten dinner before it became weird. He'd eat a slice of pizza to fit in. Some of the divorced or single mothers paid *way* too much attention to him. He's got that Vamp draw."

"Vamp draw?"

"He's a good-looking man to start with, but he also gives off this sense of power that some women are fascinated by. He tries to tamp down his allure but he can't help it. I tease him about being a chick magnet. They do seem to love him."

"Did he fool the man you were dating?"

"Yes. He didn't suspect a thing. Grandpa was kind of an ass to him though. He didn't want to be invited to more dinners. We thought it was a good plan."

"What if that relationship had grown serious?"

"It didn't. The jerk cheated on me, remember?"

Red narrowed his eyes, staring at her. "But what if the human had been faithful to you, and the relationship had grown very serious? Would you have told him the truth?"

"I never got the chance to find out."

"I'm curious, Emma. Answer the question. What would you have done if you'd married a human? You and your grandfather had to have had that discussion at some point."

She cut the steak but hesitated to take a bite. "Thomas would have figured something was off in time. I age slowly. You can say it's good genes for only so long before they start to become suspicious. I guess it would have depended on how he took the truth. Grandpa would have had to wipe his mind if he freaked out."

"So you *did* discuss it."

"Yes."

"Was your grandfather willing to allow you to marry?"

That question surprised her. "Why wouldn't he?"

"You're his nest."

"I'm his granddaughter."

"You belong to him. You said it yourself. And he's an old Vampire."

"He's a modern thinker. He hates the ancient ones who refuse to change with the times. He believes it's stupid to hold on to the past and not conform as the world progresses."

Red ate his food.

Emma focused on her own plate. "This is really good. Thank you."

Red nodded. "You're welcome. You don't think your grandfather would stop you from being with someone if you wanted to make a lifelong commitment?"

"He wants me to be happy."

"I can't see him willingly giving you up."

"I'll still be part of his life if I ever get married. I just won't live with him anymore. Grandpa could finally find a companion…I know he's lonely. I wouldn't be under his roof, which means my neck would be safe from his Vampy lover."

"How does that work? Don't Vamps get jealous when their companions feed on others?"

"I don't know. He's never had a serious lover since he rescued and raised me." She took a sip of her drink. "I can't imagine his girlfriend would enjoy watching him bite other women. I guess they could feed off each other. Or he could only bite men and she could only bite other women. That wouldn't be so bad."

"Some Vampires get turned on when they bite, regardless of which sex they're feeding from."

"I'm aware. Grandpa's only drawn to women though. We had discussions about Eduardo many times. He thinks that might be why he got so bent out of shape when Grandpa left the nest with me. Eduardo didn't just lose his master, but someone he wanted to become a companion to. Grandpa wasn't down with that."

Red chuckled. "I see."

"What's so funny?"

"Nothing."

She scowled at him. "What? Just spit it out."

"Down with that? That was kind of funny."

"No pun intended. Geez." She grinned.

"Did Eduardo confess his love or something?"

"No, but Eduardo prefers to bite men, and Grandpa often caught him having sex with his donors. Eduardo even fooled a couple into thinking it was a woman they were screwing. Grandpa gave him a stern talking to about it."

"Malachi never took sex from his victims?"

"Donors—and no, not unless they showed interest in sex before he bit them. He wouldn't take someone's free will like that. He does have morals. Eduardo didn't."

Red didn't look convinced.

Emma sighed. "Have you ever heard of Vampire brides?"

"Is that different from a companion?"

"Yes. A companion is someone you chose to be with. Your partner. A bride is akin to a blood slave. They are taken and held against their will, forced to follow orders. The master who made my grandfather collected them. He had almost a dozen. It really pissed my grandfather off."

"I don't understand."

She stopped eating, placing her silverware down. "His name was Palao. He was a piece of shit who stole women regardless of whether they were already married or had children. He'd sneak into their homes at night if they caught his interest and kill their families in front of them. They became his slaves. He liked to break their minds and spirits."

She shivered, horrified just thinking about it. "Palao kept them locked up unless he needed to use them. He'd dress them as prostitutes and throw parties for rich men in the area. He'd let those men have sex with his brides, before stealing money, jewelry, or whatever else he wanted. They'd go home only remembering having great sex and clueless about how they'd been ripped off."

Red softly growled.

"It wasn't a treat for the brides either. He pimped them out for blood and money. They weren't given a choice. Occasionally one would escape and stake herself to the ground to burn when the sun rose. Some watched that monster kill their children and husbands, helpless and stuck in that hell. If a bride pissed Palao off or didn't do what he demanded, he'd chain her to a wall and let the others watch her starve until she became raving mad from the pain, her skin stretching over her bones like a living skeleton."

Emma swallowed a lump of emotion that nearly choked her. "My grandpa said they'd suffer until they finally dried out and died from having no blood at all. He thought once they were free they might lose some of the madness created by the master. Recover. It didn't work. He had to end their suffering."

"Your grandfather doesn't have any brides?"

"Hell no! He'd never do that to someone. Ever. My grandfather watched what was done to those brides until he hated his own master. Palao's death was the best thing that could have happened to the nest. Grandpa doesn't make soldiers either, and he told anyone in his nest that he'd kill them if they ever tried. It was his number one rule. Never make an inferior Vampire. It was a killing offense."

"I know what a soldier is."

"Then you know they are more horrible than brides."

"Why?"

"Soldier are born strong but they rot away from the inside. Their minds, their internal organs, and it's just a matter of time before they go insane. They feel bloodlust all the time because they're damaged and in pain. They can't ever fully heal, regardless of how much blood they drink. There's no calm for them. A regularly fed bride remains sane and healthy for the most part. She could live hundreds of years, if not longer. The same can't be said for a soldier. You can prolong their life with regular Vampire blood feedings. They're made to kill, and usually die within half a year at most.

"A soldier without a master to feed from would maybe last a month or two and take a lot of lives before its reign of terror ended. It becomes a mindless killer, hunting anything with blood."

"How are they made? Do you know?"

Her grandfather had told her *all* the horror stories about his race. She hesitated briefly, then decided it was safe to tell Red if he gave his word to keep the secret. He wasn't Vampire enough to ever make one. He also had a heart. He was a good man who could never be cruel.

"Between us only. It goes no further. Swear?"

He nodded.

"You need to know Vampire basics to understand. Let's say I'm a Vampire and my best friend gets stabbed in the arm. I could rub some of my blood on the wound to heal it. She wouldn't turn into a Vamp from that. I could let her drink a tiny bit of my blood if she were injured, and again, it wouldn't change her. If she'd been stabbed fatally though, and was near death, she'd have to drink a lot of my blood. It would heal her, but she would turn into a Vampire. Period."

"Why are you using stabbing terms?"

She shrugged. "To save the life of a loved one is the only reason I would consider turning someone. The point is, to create a strong, healthy Vamp, they'd have to be low on blood and get enough from a Vampire to replace what they lost. They'd heal and become stronger as all that Vampire blood circulated throughout their body. It's the nature of being turned."

"Understood."

"Vamp blood heals. But imagine someone being deathly injured, given Vampire blood, but then being murdered right afterward. The heart stops beating and there's no circulation of that new blood. Vamps who create soldiers tend to do it before dawn, to make certain the corpse lays there all day before it wakes messed up. The blood is tainted by the time the new Vamp's heart begins to beat again. Parts of their bodies have, well…decayed after dying. There's no cure. It's permanent."

Red grimaced. "It sounds horrific."

"That's why my grandpa would never make a soldier. He's not evil, Red. He's a great guy. He hated his own master because he was a horrible person who became crueler as every year passed. My grandfather doesn't believe in killing unless there's no other choice, and he hates to see anyone abused. You should ask me about when he plays judge and jury."

Red arched his eyebrow.

"Sometimes he'll see a horrible crime on the news and he'll do something about it."

"Give me an example."

"There was a string of disappearances several years ago. Grandpa went to the city and talked to the police. He used his ability to control their minds to get their list of suspects and then talked to each one. He eventually found the guy. He'd used his mind control to make the guy confess. He was a real sick bastard. Grandpa had him write out where he'd left the bodies to give the families closure…and then he took him out. It looked like a suicide but he stopped a serial killer. *That's* the kind of man he is. He didn't want to read about more missing girls or see their parents on television, pleading for their safe return. He could relate to them because he always fears someone will hurt *me*.

"There was also a man accused of killing his girlfriend. I knew him well. He was a fellow student when I was still at college, a great guy. I was upset, because I really didn't think he'd done it. My grandfather met with him and discovered the truth. He was innocent. Grandpa found the killer by talking to everyone who knew the victim. It turned out to be an ex-boyfriend who hated that she was with someone else. The jerk didn't feel regret or remorse. He'd already picked out his next victim because he'd enjoyed killing her so much. Grandpa had him dig up the murder weapon, then crash his car into a tree with the weapon on the seat next to him. The police found it and cleared my friend of the crime. That bastard never got the chance to kill anyone else."

"That's a handy way to use his abilities. No one could lie to him if he entered their minds and asked questions."

"I know. My grandpa is a great guy, Red, even if he is a Vamp."

"I believe you."

She smiled, relieved. It bothered her, thinking Red might hold a grudge against her grandfather. He wasn't like most Vampires. It was important that they get along if they ever meet. She was starting to have strong feelings for Red…

She pushed that train of thought away. It made her wish for a future beyond Red keeping her safe until her grandfather lost Eduardo.

"One more question." Red held her gaze.

"Okay."

"Malachi was a part of whatever happened with the Lycans that started the war between them and Vampires. Did he tell you how that went down?"

"My grandfather tried to rule the nest after Palao died but that monster had created some shitty Vamps. They were pure bad news, used to killing humans, and they weren't going to stop. Grandpa ashed them one by one as they broke the rules, killing innocents, until he was alone. That's always dangerous. He came across another nest who offered to accept him. He liked how they got along with the Werewolves they'd made an alliance with and felt it would be a good fit."

"Lycans," Red reminded her.

She nodded. "He met my grandma and fell in love. But he was new to the nest. They didn't tell him what they were planning to do until the Vampires blatantly began to attack the Lycan women, trying to breed them like cattle. He fought the nest to protect my grandma and to help her pack escape. It's not his favorite subject to talk about. He loved her deeply, and I know it hurts him, bringing up those memories. She died almost a hundred years later."

"How? Were they attacked by Vampires?"

"No. She had gone out running in her shifted form during the day. He said she loved sunshine and would often go for runs while he slept. One day she just didn't come home. He went looking for her as soon as the sun went down. She'd been shot three times in the throat and head. He said she'd managed to get away but she must have been confused from the pain. She went over the side of a mountain and caused a rock slide. It mostly buried and crushed her. She'd died by the time he found her. It broke his heart."

"That's every man's worst nightmare."

She nodded. "It devastated him. He loved her so much."

"Did he avenge her death?"

"He hunted the man who'd shot her. It turned out it was a poor neighboring family. They were starving, and they had four small children. The man shot her while she was shifted, believing she was a something they could eat. He obviously didn't know she was a person. Grandpa let him live, even left them money for food. He would never slaughter a man for trying to feed his kids. It would have left that family without someone to protect them."

Red nodded and grew silent. She hoped he was thinking about everything she'd shared, and that his opinion of her grandfather would get better.

* * * * *

Red finished his meal and took both plates to the sink. He refused Emma's offer to wash the dishes. He had a lot of thinking to do and the chore helped him focus his thoughts.

He wanted to believe that Malachi wouldn't try to kill him if he mated Emma. She seemed certain her grandfather would just let her go and be a nice Vampire.

After a lifetime of Vamp horror stories, he'd been both relieved and confused after his discussion with his uncle. Velder seemed to like Malachi, even planned to welcome his visit without aggression when or if he came after Emma. The Vampire had helped them build Howl. It might not be the disaster he feared if he came face to face with the man.

He glanced back, watching Emma brush her fingertips over his coffee table. She seemed to really like the thing. He could take it to his cabin if she did, or he could build another one.

It had been torture to spend two days making love to her without biting. He wanted to taste her blood so bad, his gums ached. The mere thought had his dick twitching but he ignored his semi-erection. She was probably sore after going into heat. He was just grateful that it hadn't lasted long, otherwise he probably would have given in to the desire to bite her. A taste of her blood wasn't necessary, though. Not anymore.

He knew she was his mate. He'd felt it every time he'd touched her, kissed her, and held her while she'd slept.

He clenched his teeth and scrubbed a plate. He needed to convince Emma to become his mate. He didn't want to do it without her permission. She'd been raised by a Vampire, in a human world. Everything would be easier if she'd been brought up with the clan. She'd accept the mating without question once she realized what they were to each other. A VampLycan woman would have bitten him *first*, and aggressively urged him to bite her back.

The clan would accept Emma. He just had to get her to make that commitment. He'd hinted enough when they were in bed about wanting to bite her. She hadn't taken the bait by saying he could, even though she now understood why he had the urge. He should have taken her up on it the very first time she'd agreed.

He sighed. Hindsight was always obvious.

He finished cleaning the dishes and turned, walking toward Emma. "I can't believe you really made this table. It's beautiful."

"I'm good with my hands."

"I know that." She grinned.

He instantly wanted her. "Would you like to see my cabin?" He took a step closer but then stopped. Maybe viewing where she'd live if she agreed to be his mate would help his case. "It's daylight topside, and the clan is aware that you're here. Nobody comes out to my place except for some of the younger ones. They enjoy swimming in the river there. There's a natural pool and I'm an advisor to them."

"What is that in VampLycan terms?"

"A teacher." He wanted her to know he was good with kids. "All the adults pitch in to help our young learn survival skills. I have a workshop for furniture building, too, and I also work at the garage in town. I can fix anything with a motor."

"We can really get out of here?"

"For a few hours. I want us back inside the den before darkness falls."

"I don't think Eduardo is going to be able to find me. I stuck to my grandpa's plan, except for having to bribe the bus driver to bring me to Howl. It was very detailed. We've had to flee before. We're good at losing that prick when he's tracking us."

"I'd rather be safe than sorry. Has he ever had the Vampire Council help him before?"

"No. Good point. Okay, I can understand that. Nests are almost everywhere. Let's go." She almost lunged toward the exit.

"Shoes, Emma."

She halted and looked down. "Oh. Right." She grinned. "That would probably be a good idea, or I'll end up over your shoulder again."

He almost regretted pointing out her lack of footwear. He wouldn't mind carrying her. It would mean she remained close to him. She took a seat on his couch and put on the shoes that she'd stored under it. He left her there to shove on a pair of his boots. They weren't needed; years of running barefoot had left his feet pretty resilient. But he wanted to give her a good impression. It wouldn't be a bad thing to act as human as possible until she adjusted to life with him.

She was waiting by the door when he reached her side. Her excitement showed on her face, and he realized how difficult being underground must be for her. Guilt struck but she was safer inside his den. He opened the door and took her hand, leading her up and outside. The expression of joy on her face when she saw the blue sky and breathed the fresh air had him silently promising to bring her out the following day. Vamps couldn't come at her with the sun up.

"Let's stop by the river first. I need to hang the sheets to give them time to dry before dark."

"Right." She closed her eyes.

"What are you doing?"

She opened her eyes and pointed. "It's that way. I can hear the water."

Her hearing impressed him. A normal human wouldn't have been able to do that. She wasn't totally without some VampLycan traits. "You're right."

"Grandpa makes me practice using my senses."

"What else does he have you do?"

"I can fight. I'm not strong or fast enough to win if I have to duke it out with a Vamp, but I could put one down long enough to run."

He didn't like the idea of her dealing with *any* kind of violence. "How?"

Emma grinned. "You know, snap a Vampire's neck or stab them in the heart if I have something handy to use. Beheading them is better, since they die, but that's tough to do unless I have a sword or something similar. I can't exactly walk around with one strapped to my body. He taught me how to incapacitate one, to give me the opportunity to run like hell. He also taught me how to mask my scent and hide my heat signature if I'm being tracked."

"You learned how to fight with a sword?"

"Some of the older Vamps still use them. I'm skilled with one. I'm also decent with throwing knives. They're easier to hide on my body, and not having physical contact is better if I can avoid it. I'm also familiar with guns and I'm a decent shot."

"It's tough to kill a Vampire with bullets. You'd have to totally decapitate one with them."

"True but the trick is to blow enough holes in their head, throat, and heart. That bastard is going to be hurting and down for bit. It gives me time to get out of his hunting zone. Grandpa also taught me hand-to-hand combat, but as I said, I'm not good with that against a Vamp unless it's a newly turned one. Mostly, I get my ass handed to me and *I'm* the one who goes down. I don't heal as fast as my grandpa does, or you. But pain teaches me to win."

Anger filled Red, imagining anyone striking Emma. "He *beats* you?"

She scowled. "You make it sound so bad. He just makes sure that I'm not a wimp. It might save my life if someone ever comes after me."

"By striking you?"

She jerked her hand out of his and faced him. "*Stop it*. My grandpa *isn't* a bad person. Do you know how most Vamps attack? They strike quickly. Boom!" She pushed hard against his chest. "They knock you down and are on you before you knew what happened. The victims are stunned, in pain, scared. They make eye contact with their attacker and guess what happens then? Yeah. Their mind is toast, and they're lucky if they wake up alive with only a little blood loss. So *yes*, my grandpa has knocked me on my ass. He's taken me down, and I know what to do when it happens. I don't make eye contact. I attack when they least expect it. That gives me an advantage. I'm used to pain. It doesn't confuse or stun me."

He was still furious but he didn't want to upset her further. "I see."

She sighed. "It's like you're always looking for an excuse to hate him. I bet you don't train *your* youth without knocking them around. It will save their lives if you hand them their asses from time to time, right?"

He reluctantly nodded. She had a good point. "It keeps them from getting cocky and teaches them how to defend themselves better. To fight through the pain since their lives can depend on it."

"Exactly. That's what my grandfather has done for me. I need every advantage I can get. He's always been afraid something would happen to him. I'd be left on my own, adrift."

He saw the pain in her eyes. "What does that mean?"

She eased her hands off his chest. "I'm not totally human. I have to hide what I am from them. But I'm *too* human to fit in with Vampires, Lycans, or VampLycans. See where this is going? Most VampLycans wouldn't touch a human, so there probably aren't many people like me. I've never personally met one. Nobody is going to accept me, from *any* race. If Grandpa dies, I'm a boat floating on an ocean without any safe place to dock, Red. I'm alone."

"No, you aren't. My cousins are mated to women like you. Their father was human, their mother a VampLycan. You're not a boat. I'll introduce you to them when the time is right."

"When will that be?"

"Not today. We don't have *that* much time."

Chapter Eight

Emma loved being outdoors. It was a beautiful day and Alaska held a lot of wonders. She'd never been there before and she'd slept most of the trip on the bus, missing the sights. Red stayed close, his hand brushing against hers as they walked to the river. She grinned, staring at the trees and the wide stretch of water that unfolded in front of her.

Two large moose were in view downstream, drinking. "They're bigger than I imagined."

Red followed her gaze as he took a seat, removed his boots, then stood again. "Those are fully grown. Just don't wander far, Emma. There are dangers."

"Bears. I read that there are a lot of them here."

"Not many in this area. We chase them away to keep them from our homes."

She turned, gawking a little as Red removed his pants.

He smiled, taking off his shirt. "What?"

"Why are you naked?"

"I have to go in for the sheets I weighed down. I don't want to get my clothes wet."

That made sense. "Oh."

He turned his head in all directions, his gaze constantly moving. He also kept sniffing.

"What are you doing?"

"Seeking any danger to you. It's clear. Just stay put. I'll be right back."

"I won't budge."

Red waded into the water and dove under the surface. It surprised Emma. "How deep did he bury those sheets?" She inched closer to the water, waiting. Long seconds passed, turning into a minute.

Worry started to fray her nerves when Red's wet head suddenly popped up and he swam toward her, dragging the sheets behind him.

She tried to help him but he shook his head. "Stay there. Don't get wet."

Emma backed away and watched as he wadded all the sheets together and kind of gave them a tight squeeze in his arms once he had them out of the river. He walked out of the water and placed the balled material on a rock. He shook his head, sending water flying.

Cool drips landed on her and she laughed. "Jerk."

He grinned, using his hands to wipe water from his skin. "That's not the kind of wet I like to make you."

He wasn't like any human guys she'd known. His brash, bold sexual statements would take some time to adjust to. She wasn't certain how to respond but she'd welcome his touch. That much she knew.

He began to dress and she turned her attention across the river, spotting motion. Something moved in the shadow of the thickly grown trees. "Red!"

He was at her side in an instant, with just his jeans on. "What? Oh…" He smiled. "Don't worry. It's just some of our youths. I told you they come here to swim."

Two big men who appeared to be about twenty stepped into the sunlight, free of the trees. They waved—and started to strip out of their clothes.

Emma spun to give them her back, shocked. "They're taking *everything* off."

Red grinned. "VampLycans aren't shy about their bodies. Clothes would only hamper us when we swim."

"But I'm standing right here!" She refused to turn her head to peer at the duo again.

"You're with me, and word will have spread in the clan about who you are. They'll view you as one of ours."

She bit her lower lip, confused.

Red's expression sobered. "Your mother was a VampLycan. You're her daughter. It makes you clan."

That came as a surprise. "Really?"

"Yes."

She belonged somewhere? "But how?"

"I didn't know your mother was considered part of this clan once. Uncle Velder assured me that she was. That makes you clan too, Emma."

"So...I'm welcome here?"

"Yes."

"Does that mean no one would get upset if I came back in the future?"

Anger instantly tensed his features. "Yes."

"But *you* have a problem with that?"

"Why would you leave?"

She hadn't expected that response.

Red stepped closer. "You know I want to bite you. I think you're my mate, Emma."

She peered into his eyes. Was she ready to commit to him like that? It was tempting. Fear came next, though. He lived in Alaska with a VampLycan clan. He said they accepted her…but what if that wasn't really true? She needed more time to make that decision. Mating would be for life. Considering how slow she aged, and the fact that mates shared blood, their union would last hundreds of years, or even longer.

"What about your promise to your uncle, to take a VampLycan mate?"

"It's dealt with and not an issue anymore. He'd give his permission."

That downright stunned her.

"Think about it," he gruffly muttered. Then he stepped away and walked over to the discarded wet sheets. "We're going to my house. I'll just toss these in the dryer while we're there. Come on. It's a bit of a walk but I think you'll enjoy it."

Splashing sounds had her turning her head. The two men were in the water now.

She hurried after Red, following him back into the woods in a new direction, away from where they'd come out into the clearing. She had to hurry to keep up with his long strides, but it was still nice to be outdoors and moving. Her grandfather made her run for miles to keep her in shape. Fast walking was a breeze compared.

They finally exited out of thick trees into another clearing. This one was manmade though, judging by a few tree stumps she spied. A cute cabin sat in the middle of it. She smiled. It was an A-frame log structure. Red stopped at the door and punched in a code on the keypad lock. It clicked and he opened it, stepping aside. "Welcome."

"I didn't expect that on a cabin out in the middle of the woods."

"I know. Most VampLycans don't lock their doors but as I said, I work with youths. They know I have a good sense of humor. I got tired of their pranks."

"Like what?"

"The last stunt they pulled involved filling my tub with river water and fish."

That amused her. "I meant the lock. It's a keypad one. That's kind of fancy for a cabin in the woods."

"Oh. It's a pain to carry a key or hide one. In the winter, these pads can be unreliable because of the cold but in warmer weather they come in handy. Go inside."

She entered first. It had an open floorplan with beams holding up a large loft. A stone fireplace dominated one wall. The furnishings were sparse but looked comfortable. He closed the door behind her.

"What do you think? It's not very large but there's two bedrooms and a shared bathroom upstairs. I always figured I could add onto the back one day if I wanted more rooms."

"I love it." She stared at the kitchen. It was under the loft area, and a long island separated it from the living room. He'd done the kitchen in soft browns and light blues with gray stones. She walked over to the island and touched the surface. "What is this?"

"Concrete. It's tough to get marble slabs delivered here."

"It's beautiful."

"The door behind the kitchen leads to a half bath, the laundry room, pantry, and storage. It's under the other side of the loft. It looks much bigger than what you see here."

She bit her lip, studying him. "I like your home, Red. You don't have to talk it up."

"What kind of home do *you* live in?"

"Um, Grandpa's latest pick was a monstrosity of a house. Some rich guy built it, decided he didn't like living in a smaller town, and it was on the market for years. That meant he picked it up at a good price. It was a bitch to clean and all those rooms we never used were wasted space. This feels homey."

He held her gaze.

"I'm not just saying that. My favorite place out of all the homes Grampa and I shared happened to be a two-bedroom condo in a city. It was probably a thousand square feet in all. Your cabin is larger."

"Where did he sleep?"

"The walk-in closet in the master bedroom. It didn't have any windows. He was afraid to sleep in the attic space in case they worked on the roof, since it was a combined building."

"I can't see a Vampire living in a condo."

She grinned. "That was the point. No other Vampires or Werewolves, I mean Lycans, lived in that building either. It was safe, and the last place anyone would have looked for us."

"What if someone had broken in during the day?"

"Grandpa would have been pissed and taken control of their mind, had a midday snack, and sent them on their way with a bit of memory loss. Probably have them repair the door or window they broke to get inside before he let them go. He isn't helpless during the day, remember?"

Red nodded. "What about a fire?"

"Ever heard of waterproof fire safes? He bought one large enough to curl into if the need ever arose. It wouldn't have been fun for him or made him look pretty by the time I got him out, after a lack of oxygen, but he'd have survived."

Red frowned.

"Without oxygen, Vampires lose consciousness and their skin turns gray. I would have had to get ahold of that safe after the fire was put out, had it moved to a location without people around before I opened it, and had blood waiting to revive him. The smell of it would have brought him around."

"How would you get blood?"

"Animal blood would do in a pinch. Then he could go look for a human donor. I'm just glad I never had to sacrifice some pet-store bunny, since we were in a city. No cows were around to borrow some blood from. We never had a fire."

Red seemed to take that in stride. "I'm going to toss the sheets into the dryer." He disappeared through the doorway in the kitchen.

She glanced around the living space again, taking a better look at the furnishings. Everything appeared comfortable, a bit oversized, and it needed a woman's touch. Some of the tables she realized he must have made from trees. They were lovely.

And his cabin would be hers if she mated him.

Red returned and pointed at the stairs. "After you."

The loft area had her smiling. A comfortable loveseat sat next to filled bookshelves. She walked over to skim the titles. Most of the books were mysteries and action thrillers. "You like to read."

"Winters can be long."

"How do you stay warm? I know it gets very cold here."

"That storage room I mentioned gets filled with wood that I chop. Follow me."

He passed through an archway on the side that led to an open door on their immediate right. The room behind it contained a queen-size bed and dresser. He bypassed it, and the next open door revealed a bathroom. The third open door stood at the end of the hallway.

"Where I sleep."

She entered ahead of him—and immediately loved the room. It wasn't the biggest master bedroom she'd ever seen, but it was cozy. He had a king-size bed with one nightstand, a dresser, and a fireplace took up the back wall. The stones matched the ones in his living room.

"I've never seen a cabin with a fireplace on the upper floor too."

"It's the nice thing about building our own homes. We can customize them to our tastes. I like watching a fire while I fall asleep on cold nights. This beats sleeping on the couch downstairs."

"It certainly does."

"That's the tour. I'm going to grab some clothes while I'm here. I didn't expect to be staying at the den for this long."

She remembered. "You only go there on weekends. Why bother? You have such a lovely home, Red."

"There's no cell signal at the den and only two other people know where it is. Drantos and Kraven, my cousins, helped me build it. I helped them with theirs too. It's something we do in our teens. They'd never disturb me there unless it was an emergency. Let's just say that during the week, things can get hectic when it's not winter. I often need to decompress."

"I can understand that."

"What do you do for a living? Do you work?"

She grimaced. "Not currently. I'm on the run."

He stepped closer. "Before that."

"I worked for my grandfather. He's an online history professor. I mean, seriously, who knows about the past better than him? He's lived for more than four centuries of it. It sounds a bit lame to work for family, but he's not the best at learning technology. He's hired assistants but after the third one he had to fire, I took over."

"He fed on them?"

She shook her head. "They ended up with huge crushes on him. It's that whole powerful draw thing he has going on for him. I worked in a consignment shop in our last town, but I didn't mind giving it up to spend more time with Grandpa. He's fun to be around."

"He makes good money being a professor?"

"He doesn't really need the money. He's a treasure hoarder. Plus, he always bought properties wherever he lived. Then there's the antiques he'd sold off when he got rid of homes he owned a couple hundred years ago. The value of the land had also increased a lot in that time. Four-hundred-year-old Vampires tend to have a lot of acquired wealth. At least the smart ones."

"Why work at all then?"

"Teaching keeps him entertained. It's hell for me when he's bored."

"Why?"

"He tends focus too much on my life and training me." She grinned. "Never a good thing. When I was thirty-four, I called it The Year of Guns. And for my thirty-sixth birthday, he bought me four kinds of crossbows. Want to guess what I did month after month that year?"

"I've never fired one before."

"Well, if you ever want to learn, I can teach you."

"I'd like that."

A cell phone rang, and Red cursed, stalking to the nightstand where it sat charging. He disconnected the cord. "Hello, Drantos." He paused, listening.

She cocked her head, straining to hear. A faint male voice spoke, but she picked it up easily. "You were spotted heading toward your cabin. Dusti and I would like to invite you to dinner with your guest."

"I want her back in my den before dark."

"She's safe in our territory."

"I'm not going to chance it."

Drantos growled. "Dusti wants to meet Edna."

"It's Emma. And this isn't a good time for that."

"Don't make me tell Dusti no. Bat wants to meet your guest, too. They've never had an opportunity to talk to someone else like them. Both are excited to compare stories."

"Not tonight. I'm hanging up now."

"Come on, Red. Don't be a di—"

Red disconnected the call, plugged in the phone and turned, grinning. "We should return to the den."

"What was that about?"

"Nothing." He took her hand. "Let's see how the sheets are doing." He almost pushed her toward he door.

"I have good hearing, Red. Why don't you want to go to dinner?"

He growled low and stepped in front of her. "They might scare you off. Dusti is sweet but Bat can rub people the wrong way."

"But I'd like to meet other people."

He scowled.

"You said this is my clan too. That means making friends. And this Dusti and Bat have human blood, right? Their father was human? That's what you told me. I'm certain I wasn't followed here, so there should be no danger. Please?"

"We can do lunch another day. This one is almost over."

"How many VampLycans guard your territory at night? Do you think Vamps could sneak past them?"

"Hell no."

"Does this Drantos live outside of the territory?"

"No." The frown deepened.

"Come on. Call him back and say yes."

"I'm trying to keep you safe."

"I will be. *You're* with me." She grinned. "Don't make me play on your pride. You're one of those alpha types who would hate that. I'll tease you about being afraid of a few little ol' Vamps if we don't go."

He grumbled. "Fine."

"How long do you think until dinner? I've lost all track of time."

"We have a few hours."

"Fantastic! Mind if I raid your books to find a few I'd like to read?"

"You can have anything you wish, Emma."

She smiled. He could be a sweetheart.

* * * * *

Red watched Emma laugh with Batina and Dusti in Drantos's kitchen. They'd offered to do the dishes after dinner. He was glad she'd hit it off with both of his cousins' mates.

Kraven leaned forward on the couch and drew his attention. "I like her. She seems oddly pleasant for being raised by Malachi."

"Not what I had expected, either," Drantos murmured. "Father's stories implied the Vampire was rather intense. He trained the first-generation VampLycans to fight before he left."

Kraven nodded. "Dad always said Malachi wanted them prepared in case any surviving Vampires tracked them down. Some of those Vamps were old and powerful. He said he taught them how to maim and kill swiftly. I guessed his granddaughter would be highly trained but...perhaps he shielded her instead, since she's half human?"

"He trained her." Red still wasn't happy with the idea of anyone harming Emma, even if he did understand the method and reason. "Mostly with weapons, from what I gathered."

"It's for the best that she came to you for protection," Drantos said. "I can't see her fighting off Vampires. No offense."

"She smells completely human," Kraven agreed. "I've seen no hints of VampLycan from her, either."

"She has our enhanced hearing. Watch what you say." Red wasn't about to forget how Emma had overheard what should have been a private conversation with Drantos on his cell. "What did Uncle Velder tell the clan about Malachi coming?"

"He gave a description to everyone, told them he was a friend to our clan, and to politely escort him to the main house. Malachi will be staying with Mom and Dad, which means he must trust him a lot. Otherwise, he wouldn't let a Vampire near his mate." Kraven grinned. "As if Mom is helpless."

Drantos snorted. "To Dad's way of thinking, she is."

Red felt relief. "I'm glad Uncle Velder doesn't expect me to take him in."

Kraven arched an eyebrow. "Did Emma say something that makes you leery of him?"

"No. According to her, he's a hero who may as well walk on water. She gets offended when I question his motives about anything."

"Like?" Kraven leaned closer.

"She admitted he's bitten her. That pissed me off. She said it was only a few times and under emergency situations, to fool other Vampires into believing she was a blood slave."

Drantos nodded. "It would be bad if other Vampires discovered Malachi had his partial VampLycan granddaughter under his protection. Imagine what they could do if they'd captured her."

Red didn't want to. Nothing good, he was certain. "Let's go for a walk."

He stood without waiting for them and headed for the front door. Emma laughed again, looking happy. He stopped outside where they wouldn't be overheard and faced his cousins.

"What's wrong?" Kraven invaded his personal space, holding his gaze. "Whatever it is, we're family. We'll deal with it together."

"Exactly," Drantos agreed.

Red glanced at both of them. "Emma has been Malachi's only nest member for nearly forty years…I'm also certain she's my mate. She's going to hate me if I have to kill the bastard if he doesn't take the news well. He might fight me when he realizes I'm keeping her."

Kraven grinned. "First off, don't word it that way when you talk to Emma. Women hate it when we discuss them with terms of ownership. Bat's taught me that."

"Dusti's sweeter." Drantos grinned. "But agreed. Malachi will just have to deal with the loss. I got the impression Dad would welcome his visits anytime he wants. It's not as though he will be banned from seeing her forever."

Red sighed. "I still worry that he'll go for my throat, and Emma will hate me for defending myself. She loves him."

"She'll love you more if you're her mate." Kraven paused. "You sure about the mate thing? You tested her blood?"

"I didn't need to. I know. You know it's always been much more than just blood."

"Yeah. I was in denial about my instant attraction and protective instincts toward Dusti. Sometimes you just know when you meet the person you want to spend forever with. The blood is only confirmation."

Red nodded at Drantos. "I'm certain."

"Have you told her?"

Red met Kraven's curious stare. "I did. I had hoped she'd want to bond with me right away but she needs time."

"It's a big leap of faith for someone who wasn't raised hoping to find their lifelong mate. Show her how much she means to you." Kraven grinned. "And how much of a better lover you are than any human she's known."

Drantos patted his arm. "It's going to work out. Seduce her into mating with you. The bond will grow stronger after you complete it. There will be no regrets."

"Our mates will help talk her into it and be good examples. They're getting along well. Listen." Kraven jerked his thumb toward the front door.

Red cocked his head, hearing the women's continuing laughter from inside. He smiled. "I don't think Emma's had many friends, or at least, any she could completely be herself with."

Chapter Nine

Emma kept replaying in her mind the conversations she'd had with Dusti and Bat. According to them, living with VampLycans was difficult at first, but now they didn't want to be anywhere else. It was also nice to see that their human traits were as strong as hers, yet they fit into the clan. It gave her hope.

The idea of finding a home, making friends she'd never have to lie to or leave behind because she didn't age, appealed to her on every level.

Guilt filled her next though, because of her grandpa. He said Alaska held too many sad memories of her grandmother. She doubted he'd want to visit her often.

If he survived, he'd come get Emma, but would want to leave right away. That meant she'd have to make a choice. Stay with Red and her new friends or tell her grandpa she wasn't going with him. That would leave him alone in the world. Of course, he could finally find a companion. As much as she knew he loved her, he probably wanted a woman in his life who wasn't a relative.

"What are you thinking about?" Red helped Emma down the ladder that led to his den. "You've been quiet on the walk here."

"I'm great, Red. Thank you for introducing me to those guys. I love your family. They are all nice."

"That didn't answer my question."

They entered the den and he sealed the door, turning on lights. The enclosed space felt tight after being outdoors and inside the roomy cabins she'd visited. "I guess I'm just letting it sink in that I'm not the only half-human and VampLycan."

"And?" He walked up to her, gently cupping her hips.

"I like Bat and Dusti. I can't image growing up never knowing their mom was a VampLycan or that other races existed. It sounded so difficult when they realized their mates weren't human. They shared their stories with me a little. To survive a plane crash, and then learning on top of it that their grandfather was so evil...wow. I'm glad my grandpa is awesome."

"Decker was an asshole who deserved death. He's the reason I lost my father."

Horror and heartbreak surged for him. "I'm so sorry, Red." She put her hands on his chest. "You don't have to tell me what happened."

"It's all right. You should know. Decker wanted to lead all four clans. My father was attacked and murdered by someone from Decker's clan, but the assassin left evidence that pointed toward a member of Trayis's clan. Decker must have assumed my uncle would blindly attack Trayis in retaliation. We think it's why they chose my father, because he was family to our clan leader. Maybe Decker figured once he got both clan leaders out of the way, he could rule in their place. With three clans combined, he easily would have taken out the fourth. But my uncle isn't an idiot, and he and Trayis are friends. They figured out the truth together."

"You said Klackan died during a war."

"Of a sort. The war in Decker's mind between the clans. The assassin was captured and killed. He lied for Decker, swearing he acted on his own, but we knew he had been under orders."

"I'm sorry. I know it hurts losing a parent. What about your mother?"

"She's alive but…the death of my father changed her. It's rare for her to leave her home. She doesn't interact with anyone. Grief and anger have turned her bitter. She may as well have died with my father. I haven't spoken to her in a long time."

Emma slid her hands around his waist to give him a hug, holding tight. "That's got to be rough. Why don't you two talk?"

"She moved to Crocker's clan. She wants nothing to do with Uncle Velder's, Trayis's, or Decker's clans."

"Is Crocker the fourth leader of the VampLycan clans?"

"Yes. Uncle Velder, Trayis, Decker and Crocker are the original leaders. Lorn took over when Decker lost his position, and later, his life. And Lord Aveoth heads the GarLycan clan."

"Why wouldn't your mother want anything to do with them?"

"Greif made her crazy at first. She felt betrayed when my uncle didn't go to war with Trayis's clan over the loss of her mate. She accused Uncle Velder of not loving his family by refusing to avenge my father. She couldn't be calmed or reasoned with when he tried to explain he didn't believe Trayis was responsible. Long story short, she attacked my uncle, and then swore she'd kill Trayis herself. For her own safety, and to keep her from doing something rash, my uncle locked her inside her home with guards. Once the truth about Father's death finally came out…" He sighed, a look of misery on his face.

"She was embarrassed?"

He snorted and shook his head, holding her gaze. "No. She just hated everyone—including me."

"Why you?"

"She ordered me to kill Trayis when she couldn't do it herself. I trusted Uncle Velder's instincts and didn't believe that Trayis wasn't responsible. She said I chose a side, and it wasn't hers."

Sympathy welled inside Emma and she hugged him tighter, resting her head against his chest. She wanted to comfort him. His mother sounded like someone better off not a part of his life. Grief aside, what kind of woman could shun her son?

"I'm sorry."

"She lost her mate and survived, but her mind didn't. She may breathe, but the mother I knew died with my father."

"Do you have any siblings?"

"No."

That made it worse. She knew what it was like being an only child. There had been many times in her life that she'd wished for siblings.

"Drantos and Kraven are like brothers to me. We've always been close."

"That's good. I'm glad."

"And there's Peva. You met her at her store. She's family as well, just not by blood. Her older brother was very close to us until he died. We avenged Rener's death."

"Decker again?"

"No. He went on a mission but died. Vampires. Sometimes Lycan packs contact us if they're having problems they can't solve. The original pack split up when they left our lands. Some didn't travel far, others did. But they all know how to reach us. Vampires were killing humans and putting others under scrutiny. Rener went to take out the nest but they killed him instead. Uncle Velder sent in a team to avenge him. That nest no longer exists."

"Do *you* go on missions?"

"I have but not often. I'm busy enough these days with the clan. I don't need to leave." He rubbed her back. "I love holding you but I'd like to put the sheets back on the bed and grab a shower. I can still smell the river on me."

She didn't want to let him go but dropped her arms from around his waist and backed off. "I'll make the bed. You shower."

"Deal." He turned away, entering the bedroom area.

She took the sheets he'd brought back and went to work. There wasn't a question that she'd be sharing his bed. Not after he'd gotten her through her heat. The very idea of sleeping apart from him made her feel empty inside.

She bit her lip as sudden yearning hit. The idea of spending her life with him sounded too enticing. They had sexual attraction down pat. It was just outside of bed where there were still some issues. Her gaze drifted around the den and she chuckled. Issue number one would be spending her weekends underground in the confined space he seemed to love so much.

"What's funny?"

She startled and turned her head, straightening from making the bed. "That had to be the fastest shower ever." Her gaze took in his bare chest, wet hair, and the towel draped low around his hips. "You are *so* incredibly sexy."

"You are too." His eyes began to glow. He was as turned on as she was.

She bent, tearing off her shoes, her nipples beading at his growled tone. He wanted her. She didn't need to see his cock pressed against that damp towel, already knowing he'd be hard. "Red?"

"Finish stripping, Emma." He tore off the towel, throwing it to the floor, and sank down with her.

She reached for him. "Red..."

"I don't want to talk." He lifted her, put her on the bed, and tried to kiss her.

She dodged his lips and grabbed his chin, staring into his eyes. "We need to. Hold that thought."

"Why?"

"Are you really serious about wanting to mate with me?"

Some of the glow faded from his eyes and he frowned.

Shit. He didn't look pleased that she'd brought it up. "Never mind."

"Yes, I'm serious. Why? Have you made a decision?"

"Not exactly. I just wanted to discuss it more."

"*Now?*"

"Yes."

He sighed and pulled back, sitting up on the bed. "Okay. What do you want to know?"

"Are you absolutely certain I'm your mate?"

"The more time I spend with you, the greater the draw. It's tough not to bite you. The urge is there, and it's not to just test it. Inside, I know. I feel it."

"I'm drawn to you, too."

"Say yes then. Be my mate."

"I'd have to give up my grandpa. I know it would be best for him since he can finally find a woman to share his life with, but a part of me feels as if I owe it to him to ask his permission first. He gave up his nest to save my life. He's avoided other Vampires to keep me alive for the past thirty-six years. Does that make sense?"

Red nodded. "You're loyal. It's an honorable trait. While we're being honest, I worry that he'll force me to kill him."

She was horrified. "Why would you even say that?"

"You're his nest, Emma. His granddaughter. He *did* give up everything for you. What is he willing to do to keep you? You'd hate me if I was left with no choice but to kill him in the course of defending myself."

"He'll want me to be happy most of all. He'd never do that. You mean too much to me."

"Do I?"

She stared into his eyes. "Yes. Do you want the truth?"

"Always."

"I'm fighting it…but I'm falling in love with you. I think I *am* in love with you, Red. It happened so fast, but I don't want to leave with my grandpa when he comes for me, because it means I won't see you again."

Red growled and lunged, taking her down to the bed. His mouth was on hers in an instant. She gasped but kissed him back when his tongue delved into her mouth, meeting his passion. Her fingers slid into his hair as she spread her thighs, making room for him to get closer. She broke the kiss.

"Don't bite me," she warned. "I really want to do the right thing by asking my grandpa first before we make this official."

"I remember. I'll resist." He groaned, going for her mouth again.

Red stripped her as he kissed her. She loved him. That may as well be a yes to agreeing to be his mate. He just couldn't bite her until she spoke with Malachi. He respected her need to get approval of their union from her family. Hell, he'd spoken to his uncle about making Emma his mate.

He pinned her under him and trailed his mouth over her cheek to her throat. Her moans drove him insane and his dick hardened to the point of pain. He wanted inside her but he also didn't want to rush things. He ran his hands over her body had him growling. She didn't protest or seem afraid when he made such rough sounds.

She *was* his mate. He inhaled her scent, knowing. He felt it down to his damn bones and through every beat of his heart. *Mine.*

His fangs elongated, and he salivated, desperate to bite into her, to just get a small taste of her blood, but he resisted. There would be no turning back for him once he broke skin. Instinct would overpower him, forcing him to claim her. As much as he wanted that, he wanted her happy more. That meant waiting for the right time. It wasn't now.

He tore his mouth away to be less tempted to bite and got to his knees. He rolled her over, grabbed her hips, and helped her get on her hands and knees in front of him. Emma flipped her hair out of her face and peered at him over her shoulder. He glanced down at her luscious ass and growled again.

She spread her legs apart and arched, teasing him. Worse, she rocked a tiny bit to mimic what it would look like if he were fucking her. The scent of her arousal filled his nose. She smelled unbelievable…hot and ready for him. Needy. His skin tingled and he had to pull in a sharp breath to keep fur from sprouting.

"Don't tempt me to partially shift, Emma."

She stilled, her eyes widening. "What does that mean?"

"Half state. Human form with some fur. I don't want to frighten you but you turn me on that much." He attempted to joke, to lighten the mood and cool his lust down. "Don't tempt the beast to come out to play."

He expected her to crawl away or maybe express fear, but she did neither.

"Show me."

"What?" He couldn't have heard her say that.

"Show me, Red."

"I don't want to scare you."

She smiled. "You don't. Show me, please? I'm curious."

He hesitated but then allowed some fur to sprout along his arms, chest, and down his body. He gripped her hips with his hands as his claws slid out, gently, to avoid digging them into her skin. It was tough to prevent the bones in his face from changing but he managed. A snout would be bad. He didn't think she would like that look at all.

Red watched her as her gaze slid over him, again expecting her fear.

Instead she smiled, shocking the hell out of him.

"That's kind of sexy." She lifted a hand and reached back, running her fingers lightly over his arm and the back of his hand. "Not exactly bunny soft, but hot. I still want you."

"Fuck," he snarled, inching closer to her and spreading his legs on the outside of hers to line them up right. She was much shorter. His dick was so hard and he didn't need to let her go to press the tip against her wet sex.

He slowly pushed forward, entering her.

She moaned and looked away, dropping her head. "Your cock feels even hotter and thicker."

His mate wasn't afraid of him. Pure joy and a rightness filled Red as he sank deeper into her wet, tight pussy. "Tell me you want it fast and hard." He wasn't sure he could give it to her any other way.

"Yes!" she moaned.

That was it. He gripped her hips a little tighter, still careful with his claws, and began to thrust deep and fast, taking her. Instinct rode him to bite but he refused to curl over her back and sink his fangs into her skin.

Just the thought of sampling her blood, how warm and luscious it would taste, and making her drink his own, had Red almost coming.

He slid a hand down, twisted his wrist, and used his knuckle to furiously rub her clit. Her pussy clamped tighter around him, her moans growing louder, and he held on to his control until she screamed out his name.

He closed his eyes, threw back his head, and damn near howled when his seed began to shoot inside his mate.

He wanted to get her pregnant. He wanted to seal their bond. He'd kill anyone who ever tried to take her away.

"Mine!" he roared.

When his mind cleared, he gently withdrew and rolled her onto her side. He followed her down, wrapping his still half-shifted body around hers. She snuggled back into him as he spooned her.

"You feel so right in my arms, Emma."

"You're home to me, Red. That's what it feels like." She ran her fingers over his arms and then twisted. He released her as she turned, facing him. She petted his chest, exploring him. He held her gaze when she looked into his eyes.

"This doesn't scare you?"

"No. It's a part of you. Is this as much as you shift?"

"No."

"Can I see?"

Would she be terrified? It chilled him to the bone, the thought of her rejecting him after she saw him fully shifted. "VampLycans don't look like wild wolves."

"I've seen Werewolves before. Grandpa pointed some out to me one night."

"We don't look like them, either. The Vampire blood makes us more humanoid, with less hair."

She reached up and stroked his cheek. "Show me, Red. I'm not going to freak out. I trust you. Do the same."

He nodded, hoping he wouldn't regret it. "Let me go."

She wiggled away from him and he sat up, then rolled onto his hands and knees. "Ready?"

"Yes."

He closed his eyes and shifted the rest of the way. His bones reshaped, popping and cracking. He inwardly winced at the sounds his body made. He didn't dare look at her to see her reaction until it was over.

She hadn't moved away. He could hear her breathing.

Red opened his eyes, staring at Emma.

She once again shocked the hell out of him by giving him an incredible smile.

"That is *amazing*!" She crawled right up to him, stood on her knees, and gently cupped his head. "Your eyes turn completely black and it make you look totally kick-ass. That's so cool. And pointy ears! Can you move them?"

He twitched his ears. She laughed, then maneuvered to his side. Emma ran her hands through his fur, exploring his shoulders and back. "You've got a lot of muscle still, Red. You're way beefier and bigger than a Werewolf. Sorry. Lycan." She laughed again.

He turned his head, watching her. He would have smiled if he could have.

Instead, he shifted back to skin and lunged for her, taking her down and rolling at the same time to make sure she landed on top.

"I love you, Emma. Thank you for accepting me."

She laughed. "I love you too." Her expression sobered. "Seriously, Red. I accept you for who you are. All of you. But no way are you ever fully shifting and fucking me."

His eyebrows shot up. "I wouldn't ask."

"That's a relief." She smiled again. "A little fur is hot but the snout is a mood killer for sex. Plus, the four legs. I like your hands on me. Not paws with claws."

"I only lost some of my skin because of instincts. I want to mate you badly. The urge is getting stronger."

"My grandpa will hopefully come soon."

He saw worry in her eyes, and sadness.

"He will," he assured her.

Emma snuggled into him. "I just worry."

"I know." He ran his hands down her back, caressing her gently. "He'll come and everything will be fine." He just hoped he wasn't lying.

Chapter Ten

Red jerked awake, his senses screaming something wasn't right.

A light thump came from somewhere. His hold on Emma tightened and he rolled, pinning her under him. He lifted his hand, covering her mouth as her body tensed under his.

"Shush," he breathed. "Someone is above."

She clutched at him but nodded.

"Not a sound," he warned. "Don't move." He rolled off her, got to his feet, and unleashed his claws. Hair sprouted along his body but he kept his human shape.

A light tap sounded on metal. His keen hearing picked it up. He moved out of the bedroom, through his living space to the door that led to the stairwell. His den wouldn't be breached but he'd kill anything that tried to get to his Emma.

Tap. Pause. *Tap. Tap. Tap.* Pause. *Tap.* Pause. *Tap. Tap. Tap.* Then six quick ones.

He relaxed and allowed his body to shift completely to skin. His claws retracted.

"I'm turning on the lights and we're getting dressed, Emma. It's Kraven. He's at the upper hatch. Something is wrong."

"What is it?"

He spun, flipping on lights to help her see. "I don't know but he's at the upper hatch for a reason. He'd only come to my den in case of an emergency."

"Shit." She shoved off the covers, exposing her nudeness, and scrambled for her clothes. "There's no way I led Vampires here. I was very careful."

Red threw on a pair of jeans and a T-shirt. He made sure Emma was mostly dressed before he stormed to the hatch, unlocked it, and began to climb. He unlocked the upper one.

Kraven flipped it open and met his gaze. "Sorry. Dad sent me."

"What's happened?"

"A call came through the gas station. It was a female, race unknown, but she left a message for Emma from her brother Mal."

"Damn. What was the message?"

Kraven shrugged. "Dad didn't tell me, Red. I just got a call. He told me that much, and then asked me to immediately escort you both to his house."

Red nodded. "We'll be right up."

"You're not going to invite me in?" Kraven grinned. "It's been a while since you showed the place off."

"Do you want to smell sex?"

"I'll wait outside." Kraven disappeared.

Red climbed back down and entered his den. Emma had finished getting dressed. "Put on your shoes."

"What's going on?"

"I'm not sure. Some woman left a message at the gas station for you, from your 'brother Mal.' I don't know what words were said. Uncle Velder wants us at his house now."

It only took them a minute to put on shoes. He went out first and locked the hatch at the top of the stairs. He exited the hill that covered his den, momentarily blinded by the bright sunlight. He reached back, knowing Emma would have the same problem. She clutched his arm. Kraven waited ten feet away.

Red kept hold of her as they started to walk. She slowed them down but he knew she didn't enjoy traveling over his shoulder. The terrain would also be too rough to hold her in his arms, since they had to climb a few ravines. He did scoop her up when they crossed a stream, not wanting her to get wet. He put her down on the other side.

"My brother Mal," she muttered. "That means whoever called must be human."

"How do you figure that?" Kraven glanced back at her.

"Humans are the only ones who think he's my brother. He looks too young to be my father."

"It will be fine," Red assured her.

She clutched his hand tighter. "I feel like I'm going to be sick. What can this mean?"

"I don't know. We'll hear the message and hopefully figure it out. We're almost to Uncle Velder's."

Red worried about Emma. Kraven reached the front door first and opened it, walking inside. Red followed, keeping Emma close. Uncle Velder sat on the couch with Drantos seated in a chair to his right. Aunt Crayla came from the kitchen with a tray of refreshments.

He relaxed. She'd only bother with drinks if the situation weren't as tense as he feared.

"Emma, I'd like to introduce you to my uncle Velder and aunt Crayla. He's our clan leader." He put her in front of him but wrapped an arm around her waist, pulling her against his chest. He wanted his family to know how much she meant to him. Not that the scents coming off them both wouldn't be a hint. They hadn't taken the time to shower. Everyone would know their relationship had grown serious.

"Hello." Emma sounded nervous. "It's nice to meet you."

He rubbed her stomach through her shirt and leaned his head down to put his lips close to her ear. "They're family. Relax."

Aunt Crayla sniffed as she set the tray on the table then straightened, assessing Emma before she met his gaze. "I see the men in our family all have a preference."

He knew what she implied. Her sons had chosen half-humans to mate. Now *he* had as well. He tensed. Aunt Crayla smiled though and took a seat next to her mate, curling into his side. Red let out a long breath of relief, steering Emma toward the loveseat.

Uncle Velder got right down to business by addressing Emma. "A woman called the gas station to leave a message for you." He paused. "She refused to give her name but said to tell Emma that her brother Mal is searching for her and to please get in contact. She hung up after that. My people know of you, so the one who took the call contacted me immediately. We traced it to a library in California. Does this mean anything to you?"

"We lived in California for a while. One of our neighbors, a woman, worked at a library." She gave the name of it.

Uncle Velder nodded. "That's the one."

Red turned his head, studying Emma. She appeared pale and she chewed on her bottom lip. She met his gaze. "Remember the woman who ended up with the mailman? That's her. I don't know how Linda would know to call here. We haven't spoken to her since we left California."

"Is there any way the Vampires would have known she'd been one of your grandfather's donors?" He was proud he'd used that term instead of victims, not wanting to make her upset.

She shook her head. "I don't see how. And we left there because of a Werewolf pack." She glanced around. "Sorry. Lycan pack. A couple of them came into my work and I caught their interest. Then two of them tried to follow me home, but I was able to lose them by going to a mall and abandoning my car for a cab. Grandpa said they probably picked up his scent on my clothes from hugging me and maybe thought I was being fed on. It was time to go."

Kraven frowned. "How did you know they were Lycans?"

"The way they were watching me and how they moved. It was clear that they weren't human, and Vampires don't stroll into stores during broad daylight. That left Lycan. Plus, one guy kept sniffing when he got close. Big tipoff. I hit the mall, called Grandpa, and he packed our place. I rented a motel room for the night, and then we flew out of there on separate flights."

"Focus on the message this woman left at the gas station," Uncle Velder advised.

Emma nodded. "Okay. It doesn't make sense though. Grandpa knows *exactly* where I am. He isn't searching for me." She paused. "Wait a minute...we always had an emergency plan if we were ever separated. I need to use your phone."

Uncle Velder frowned. "What was the plan?"

"We've always owned one house that we never lived in. Grandpa bought it when I was a kid. He had a phone turned on there and an answering machine installed. It was somewhere no one could trace us to but we could leave messages on the machine for each other. He changed the number over the years but he always made me memorize it, and the code. That's the only thing I can think to try, because again, he knows where I am. It's even more confusing if the caller was Linda. It's been like twenty-two years since we saw her."

Red wished he had an answer. He held his uncle's gaze. "What do you think?"

Uncle Velder stood, walked out of the room toward his office, and returned moments later. "We keep a few untraceable cell phones. Do it." He offered it to Emma. "On speaker, please."

She accepted it. Red noticed her hands trembled as she figured out how to operate the phone and dialed. She hit speaker. They heard it ring, then a computerized message played and Emma punched in numbers. It beeped and gave her options. One message had been left.

He saw dread and fear flash across her features as it started to play.

"Emma," a male voice said clearly. "The council left and I've killed Eduardo. He'll never be a problem again. As soon as you get this message, you need to return home. Everything is fine. I miss you, Princess. Come home as soon as you can. I love you."

The message ended.

Red watched Emma turn off the phone, tears spilling over her cheeks.

"Well, it seems the situation is over." Uncle Velder crossed his arms. "That's good."

Emma violently shook her head and more tears slid down her face. "No, it's not. Shit!" She stared up at Red. "He's in trouble."

"What's wrong?"

"Where do I start?" She sat the phone on the coffee table. "He called me Emma."

"That's your name, isn't it?" Drantos asked.

"Yes, it is. We have code words, though. Using my name means it was a forced call. He'd have used one of his pet names for me if he wasn't under duress."

"He called you princess," Kraven pointed out.

"Princess is code for 'prisoner.' He also called Eduardo by his name. If he'd said, 'I killed that annoying asshole,' well...you get the point." She wiped at her tears, focusing on Red. "They have him at the house. They're keeping him against his will and forced him to make that call. Everything in that message meant the exact opposite. He's telling me *they* want me, and to stay away. And the council is there too. Otherwise, he'd have referred to *them* as 'those interfering asswipes,' or something along those lines. He hates the council. And he said goodbye... He thinks they'll kill him. I have to do something!" Panic sounded in her voice and he could see it in her eyes.

"I'm curious about something," Aunt Crayla murmured. "I believe you...but why does princess mean prisoner?"

Emma turned to his aunt and sniffed. "Grandpa used to read me fairy tales. We used to joke that every princess was always kept prisoner. It seemed like a running theme. I never wanted to be a princess growing up. It meant being locked up."

"Ah. I didn't know that. I only had boys. They weren't into fairy tales."

Emma sniffed again and turned to Red. "I have to go to Oregon. I can't just let them kill him!"

Terror instantly hit. "No fucking way. That's what they want."

"They're going to kill him!" She clutched his hand. "Grandpa would do anything to save me. I have to do the same. I could go in around noon. Most of them aren't strong enough to wake while the sun is up. Eduardo isn't, at least not when he was in Grandpa's nest. Before I fled, Grandpa said the ones from the council were young. I might have to deal with any humans they forced to defend them during the day but I'm faster than they are. Stronger. My fighting skills are good enough, and we have weapons stashed on the property. I'll go in armed. I could get Grandpa out by wrapping him in blankets and lead him to the garage. He'll fit in the trunk of the car I left behind, and I'll drive him out of there. We'd be long gone before they wake and try to come after us."

Red shook his head. "No. He wanted you to stay away."

"I know," she pleaded. "But how can I just leave him? No one will help him if *I* don't. I'm all he has."

"It would be suicide if you went alone." Uncle Velder glanced at his sons before smiling at Red. "We owe Malachi. I have a plan. Are you thinking what I am, Glacier? Mandy?"

A couple came out of the hallway that led to the office. Red frowned at the GarLycan and his mate. "What are they doing here?"

"Listening at my request in case they were needed, since this mess involves the Vampire Council." Uncle Velder cleared his throat. "Mandy, tell her why she's wrong about the Vampires the council sent, please."

Mandy nodded. "Those Vamps that showed up at your place may have been young, but they have the ability to move during daytime under the cover of a building. You'd walk inside and get the shock of your life when you came face to face with them. The council only sends assassins…and they're fed blood from the masters to give them that ability. They'd be too easy to kill if sun put them out of commission all day."

Emma sagged against Red. "Are you sure?"

"You could say I'm an expert on the council and how they work." Mandy glanced at her mate. He gave a slight shake of his head. Red knew why. Glacier didn't want his mate to admit she used to be one of those very assassins.

Mandy faced Emma again. "I've dealt with them before. The real question is, why do they want *you*, Emma? You're part human and VampLycan, right? Do you have any special abilities?"

"No. My mom was VampLycan, my father human. I heal faster than a human, don't age the way they do, have heightened senses. Hearing and smell. No shifting abilities at all or Vampire traits. I'm stronger and faster than a human but would get my butt handed to me in a fist fight with a Vampire or Lycan." Emma wiggled her hand. "I have no claws."

"Give me your best guess, Mandy." Uncle Velder stood, passing out drinks. "Let's hear it."

Mandy didn't take a glass. "She doesn't belong to one of your clans."

"She does," Uncle Velder corrected. "But the council wouldn't know that. She didn't either, until I told Red her mother was one of ours before she left Alaska with her parents. That makes her one of mine, since she's here. I accept her."

Mandy nodded. "Okay. They *think* she's without a clan, therefore they'd believe she has no protection, and she's weak enough for them to control." Mandy frowned at Emma, seeming to study her. "She's attractive. Two things come to mind. One, someone is thinking of breeding her to see what the result would be, or two, they plan to use her as leverage after that little meeting on the roof they had with my mate. They can offer her up as a peace offering if they fuck up again to avoid bringing the wrath of GarLycans down on their asses."

Red snarled, enraged. "They aren't touching her."

Mandy pressed against her mate. "Calm down, Red. Don't get mad at me for saying it aloud. I'm with you all the way. I'm just tossing out ideas on why they'd bother to help this Eduardo asshole to go after her and his master. Then again, the council might want her to control Malachi. I don't know why though. He's what? Four hundred? I could see it if he were a few thousand years old. They'd cream their jeans to get control over an ancient, and definitely use Emma to make him do what they want."

Emma stilled. "His master was thousands of years old."

Mandy cocked her head, regarding Emma with a frown. "What was his position in the nest with his master?"

"He was second-in-command." Emma lowered her gaze.

Red picked up on her pounding heart and the faint scent of fear came off her. He held her tighter, glancing around. Everyone in the room seemed to pick it up too. They all knew she was hiding something.

"Emma, you need to tell me everything," Mandy coaxed. "I can't help you figure this out if you don't. What was his real position in the nest? Was he their historian? Perhaps he has information they want to force out of him."

Red growled. "Leave it be."

Uncle Velder snarled. "Shut up, Red. The council wants something from Malachi, and we need to figure out what that is. Those bastards don't do anything without a motive that usually means trouble for others."

He nodded and took a deep breath. "Trust us, Emma. Tell them."

She turned her head and stared at him. "I don't want to get him in trouble."

"Your grandfather?"

She gave a sharp nod.

"Trust our clan," Red begged. "Please?"

"It's important," Mandy urged. "Is this related to the original Vampire and Lycan war? We recently got word that they were going after a Vamp associated with it. Does he know something that could do harm to the VampLycans?"

Emma blinked away tears and broke eye contact with Red, turning her attention on Mandy. "Grandpa *did* become second-in-command. He did anything he could to gain the trust of his master, to get Palao to feed him a lot of his blood. It was the only way to get strong enough to survive him in a fight for more than a minute or two. My grandpa drained his ass when he had a chance…and then he ashed Palao by taking his head.

"It's against the law to kill your maker. It wasn't back then, but it's a death sentence now." Emma sucked in a breath. "Palao was a vicious, vile son of a bitch who got off on killing and tormenting people. His own and humans. Maybe he had friends or something that now sit on the council. Maybe they just don't like it that my grandfather refuses to deal with them. He's anti council."

Mandy grimaced. "I can see them being petty enough to do that just out of revenge for Malachi being on the VampLycan side of the war. What I don't understand is how they even *got* Malachi if he drained his master. He'd be pretty damn strong and fast if he drank that much from a master who was thousands of years old. A team of assassins should be no problem."

"I don't know."

The sadness in Emma's voice hurt Red to hear. He reached out and scooped her up, setting her on his lap. "We're going after Malachi, then?"

Uncle Velder nodded. "We owe him. He helped the original pack escape from the Vampires who attacked our Lycan families. My mother survived because of him, along with all the firstborns."

"We warned the council to be choosier about who they sent their assassins after." Glacier shrugged. "They should have listened."

Mandy stared up at her mate. "That wasn't the exact threat."

"Are you defending them?" Glacier scowled at her.

"No way. I'm not a fan of theirs."

Kraven cleared his throat. "Is it possible they know that Malachi is the only Vampire that we'd allow to walk into our territory? Perhaps they want to turn *him* into an assassin and use his granddaughter as leverage to force him to kill."

Mandy faced him. "They were pissed when the GarLycans gave them a warning. They don't like to be reminded that they aren't at the top of the food chain. But Malachi's association is with VampLycans. Not Lord Aveoth's clan." She frowned. "Then again, the two clans work together and are closely aligned. Maybe they think it will send a message to Lord Aveoth to back off. The council are such dicks sometimes."

"It doesn't matter what their motives are. They can't use Malachi if we take him from them." Uncle Velder glanced around. "VampLycans never forget a debt. He was there when we needed him. We'll be there for him now."

Emma turned her face against Red's chest and he felt her warm tears seeping through his shirt. He rubbed her back and placed a kiss on her head.

"I need to go with them, Red."

"Yes, you will," Uncle Velder agreed.

Red snarled, glaring at his uncle. "No! Emma stays here, where she's safe."

"I'm sorry, but they're expecting her, Red. They might kill Malachi if they see us instead of Emma. She needs to distract them to allow us time to surround wherever Malachi is being held. I have a plan, but she needs to be part of it."

"No way." Red wouldn't allow her to be in danger.

Uncle Velder growled. "They want her alive. That means she should be safe until we can take control of the situation. We'll send her in and while they're focusing on her, we'll slip in to attack."

"I'm *not* willing to risk her." And he wasn't. He'd just found his mate. No way in hell would he lose her.

"Damn it, Red! Think with your head instead of your heart. I'm not talking as your uncle but as your clan leader. We'll give these bastards what they want—and so much more. Emma is clan. You think I'd let her walk into a trap unless I was sure we could get her out again?"

Red's anger boiled over into rage. He refused. No way would he allow Emma to go on this mission.

Emma sniffed and jerked her face away from Red's chest. His eyes had turned pitch black and fur had sprouted on his face. He looked utterly out of control.

"I'm going, Red."

"*No.*"

"It's my grandpa. We have some secret passages in the house. They can sneak in before anyone inside figures out I didn't come alone. I *am* going." She wasn't about to let him talk her out of it.

"I won't allow you to be bait!"

She flinched at that term. "Not bait. A distraction. Listen to your uncle. He's right. They could kill my grandpa outright if I don't show up. They need me to use against him."

Red picked her up and sat her on the couch next to him. He stood, snarling loudly, turning to glare down at her. "You can't fight Vampires! What's to say they don't kill *you* once they know you aren't alone? You just said they'll kill Malachi if you don't show up."

She refused to cower, getting to her feet. "Stop trying to intimidate me. I see that you're pissed but he's my *grandpa*!"

"You're my mate!"

"Not yet. I haven't agreed. And I won't if you make me chose between you and Grandpa. Please don't do that, Red. I love you…but I owe him everything. I'm alive because he saved me. My mom died for the same reason."

"Then you should know he'd also be willing to die for you. He doesn't want you to go near that house. You said it yourself."

He was right. She didn't deny it. "I was always bad at doing everything he expected of me. I've got to try to save him. Even if it turns to shit and I die. I couldn't live with myself if I didn't try. *Please* understand that, Red." She stared into his eyes and softened her voice. "I couldn't live with it," she repeated.

Red closed his eyes and his shoulders slumped. Then he spun, storming toward the front door. She watched as he yanked open the door and left, slamming it hard behind him.

"He'll calm down," Velder sighed. "Give him time."

She turned to him, refusing to let her tears fall. "What's the plan?"

"Send you in, let them think they've won, and then attack the fuckers. Simple plans are always the best, in my experience."

She nodded. "Do you have paper? I need to draw out the house, the layout, and where the secret passages are. One runs behind the wall from the basement to the roof. There's also a tunnel from the property next door that leads to the wine cellar in the basement. It was a bitch to dig out and you'll have to crawl through it, but Grandpa always liked to keep our options open when we decided to settle into a home on a long-term basis."

"That will make it easier."

She stared at Glacier. "Are you family to Red too?"

"I'm a GarLycan." He touched the woman next to him. "This is my mate, Mandy. We live with the VampLycans."

"They're part of our clan now," Velder informed her. "Part of *your* clan."

Emma tried not to stare at the GarLycan but failed.

"What?" Glacier grinned slightly, cocking an eyebrow.

"Half Gargoyle, right? I didn't know your kind existed. You remind me of a Lycan with your size though, and with the way you move."

"You should see him shifted. He's got wings." Mandy winked at her. "It's really cool to see, yet terrifying. His body also hardens on demand until his skin becomes armor. Bullets bounce right off."

Emma let that information sink in. "What are *you*? I mean, if you don't mind me asking. You smell like your mate."

"You could say I've got a lot of GarLycan in me." Mandy grinned. "Leave it at that."

"Okay." Emma knew when to stop prying. Her gaze drifted to the door. "Should I go after Red?"

"No. Give him time to calm down. He will return soon." Velder approached her. "Let's go in my office. You can start filling us in on the property to give us every advantage we can get. I'm glad for paranoid Vampires right now, if Malachi has an escape tunnel. That sounds better than storming it from above ground."

Emma followed him. So did the tall GarLycan and both of Velder's sons. The other women stayed in the living room.

Velder took a seat behind his desk and waved Emma to a chair. He opened a drawer and removed paper, passing it to her. Then a pencil. "Draw the layout of the house and land first."

Emma got busy.

Glacier spoke next. "You can go in from the basement. I plan on coming in from the air."

Velder turned to Glacier, frowning. "It will be daylight. We can't risk humans seeing you."

"We'll figure it out. Did you think I'd sit this one out? I fucking told the council to be pickier about who they send their people after. I think it's time to give them a reminder. VampLycans and GarLycans are allies. They want Emma." He fished out his phone. "I bet a few of my brothers have some free time. We might as well make this a party. Fun times."

Emotion choked Emma. "Thank you." She took time to meet every pair of eyes in the room. "Seriously. Thank you. It's always just been me and my grandpa. I appreciate you helping me save him. However this turns out, I want you to know that."

Velder nodded. "You're Red's mate, even if you haven't let him claim you yet. That makes you family as well as clan."

Tears filled her eyes, but she blinked them back, nodding.

Chapter Eleven

Emma felt nervous. Red wasn't helping, sitting two rows up and on the other side of the aisle in the commercial passenger van that a Lycan named Graves had picked them up in. Their group had flown on a few small planes that dropped them off at a larger airport, where they'd boarded a private jet that had taken them to Oregon. She was bone tired and just wanted to curl up on his lap.

He kept his distance though, still angry that she'd refused to stay behind.

Nine VampLycans, plus her, and the Lycan driver, were traveling in the bus. Glacier had left them once the jet had landed to meet up with one of his brothers. They'd all stay at a hotel, spend the night there, and attack at noon tomorrow.

She wanted to immediately go to the house but the sun had gone down. Velder ordered her to be patient and reminded her it would give them an advantage to attack midday. Eduardo would be down during the daytime, and the council assassins wouldn't be able to leave the shelter of the house.

"It's going to be fine," Velder assured her, sitting next to her.

"Red's still mad," she whispered. "He won't even look at me."

"His anger is directed at me. Not you. He came, didn't he? It's because you're his mate."

She looked at him. "Thank you again for doing this."

"I would have preferred to leave you behind, except I fear the Vampires will kill Malachi in retaliation if you're *not* there. You need to get close enough to your grandfather to let him know an attack is about to happen. I hate to send you in at all, but we do need them focused on you. Make a hell of a scene or something. Just distract them. We'll have surprise on our side."

"I can do that. I hope you capture Eduardo. I've got a lot to say to him and none of it will be nice. I'm down with screaming at him. He's the reason my mom is dead."

"Just don't encourage him to attack you. We've gone over the plan. Just stall as long as you can to keep them unaware." His voice deepened. "Don't rush inside, regardless of their tactics. Understand? Approach slow to give us time to make it through that tunnel."

She nodded. "I know. Believe me, I know."

"The less time they have you, the less harm they can do."

A snarl sounded from Red.

Emma peeked his way. He didn't glance back but it was obvious he could hear their conversation. She sighed, looking at Velder again. He winked.

She was glad *he* seemed amused. She wasn't. All she wanted to do was be close to Red. Sure, he'd come along on the trip, but he hadn't touched her once since he'd stormed out of his uncle's house. Travel arrangements had been hurried, then they'd left within an hour after she'd drawn up the maps, driving off VampLycan territory to meet up with human pilots.

Red had hovered nearby, always. That had to mean something. He'd insisted on flying on the same small plane as she had. Sitting in the front instead of the back with her. It irritated her, more than anything. Why didn't he just yell and then let them work it out?

The bus pulled up at the hotel. Velder gripped her arm as the driver got out, keeping her in her seat. "Let Graves go in first. We don't want to alert any Vampires that we're here. He'll make sure it's only humans inside and then we'll get our rooms."

"Who is this Graves? Is he part of our clan?"

"No. He's family to some of the clan though and works for us at times. His alpha is half-brother to Trayis. He's another clan leader."

"I'll pay whatever he's asking to help us."

"No need." Velder released her and grinned. "Graves volunteered for the job. We reached out to his brother first, to be our scout. They were together, and not too far from here on vacation. Micah is probably already inside the hotel."

"I'll thank both of them then."

He chuckled. "They might thank *you* instead. Both love a good fight, and it's rare for me to leave Alaska. They didn't want to miss this."

She hadn't even thought about that. "I'm so sorry! You're away from your mate."

"Crayla knows this is important. Glacier made the GarLycans' position clear during a conversation with the Vampire Council. Now I want to personally send a message of my own. You're part of my clan and under my protection. The bastards are going to learn not to fuck with one of mine."

A slight shiver ran down her spine at his cold tone. She wasn't afraid of him—but she almost felt sorry for the council.

Worry came next. All the things that could go wrong started to play in her mind. VampLycans were damn hard to kill though. Mostly, it was her and her grandfather's lives on the line. She wouldn't feel bad if Eduardo and the Vampires with him were slaughtered.

"The Lycans are tough?" She didn't want them to get hurt.

"Graves is a judge for his alpha and other packs. He taught Micah how to fight. I'm not worried."

"What's a judge?"

Velder lowered his voice. "Graves is a nickname he's earned."

She let that sink in. He killed people for his pack. She swallowed and nodded. "Okay."

The side van door opened and Graves smiled. "Humans only in the hotel. Let's go. Micah already got you rooms and will pass out keys at the elevators. They have room service until midnight if you're hungry. You should avoid the bar and restaurant, just in case a Vamp wanders in looking for a meal."

Emma allowed Graves to help her out. He winked and she ducked her head. He was a handsome yet intimidating guy. She wasn't used to being around Lycans. Then again, she wasn't used to being around VampLycans, either.

She turned, watching Red get out. He met her gaze briefly but then passed her, stomping into the hotel ahead of her.

She sighed, following.

It was easy to identify Micah. There was a family resemblance to Graves. She allowed the men to greet him first before walking up to him. He had pretty eyes and a nice smile. He didn't hand her an envelope with a keycard, but instead pointed to Red, already standing at the elevators.

"He has yours."

"Thank you." She paused. "For helping and everything."

He winked too. Maybe it was a Lycan thing. "No problem. See you tomorrow. My brother and I are going to hang out in the bar to keep an eye on things." He lowered his voice. "To make sure no one shows up who shouldn't be here."

She nodded and turned, walking to Red. He still looked angry, but he didn't avoid her gaze. "Micah said you have my key."

"*Our* key." He turned away and punched the button for the elevator.

The other men were around them, also waiting for elevators. She sealed her lips but was surprised to find out they were sharing a room. *This should be interesting. He isn't even speaking to me.* She bit back a sigh and got into the elevator when it opened. Velder and a VampLycan named Lake went to the fifth floor with them. All of them got out, and she noted their rooms were in the same area.

She followed Red to a door and he opened it, waving her in.

She walked inside and flipped on the lights. The room had two queen beds. "I guess we're not sleeping together."

He closed the door and engaged the inside bar. "Micah got everyone the same setup in their rooms. Some are sharing."

She turned to stare at him. "Can we talk about what's wrong now?"

He reached up and ran his fingers through his shaggy hair. "I'm pissed."

"No shit. Sulking and avoiding me isn't the way to deal with this, though."

He growled and his eyes narrowed.

"What? That's what you've been doing."

"I'm not going to fight with you." He slid past her and walked to the desk. "Here's the room service menu. You need to eat." He spun, thrusting it at her. "Find what you want and I'll order us dinner."

She took it, glanced at the options, and picked one. "We need to work this out, Red."

"I said I'm not fighting with you." He took the menu and went to the phone on the desk, lifting it. She used the bathroom while he spoke to someone to place their order. She stared at her reflection while she washed her hands and splashed some water on her face. A shower was in order. She stripped, not bothering to tell Red what she was doing. He would figure it out.

It wasn't until she'd dried off that she realized she hadn't grabbed her bag from the van. She wasn't even sure what was inside it. There had been no time to go to the den. Mandy, Glacier's mate, had brought it before they'd loaded up to go meet the small planes. They were about the same size.

She just wrapped a towel around her body and exited the bathroom. Red sat in a chair at the table, arms crossed, and eyes closed. He looked tired. She approached him.

He tensed. She halted.

"I'm not fighting with you," he muttered. Yet again.

"Fine. I forgot my bag."

He opened his eyes and pointed toward the door. "Graves dropped them off. Getting inside our rooms as fast as possible was the priority. We don't want our scents lingering in the lobby."

She turned and walked to the door. Two small bags sat there, just inside. She lifted the borrowed one from Mandy and paused at the bathroom door. "This is the plan? No talk?"

He growled low.

Her temper snapped and she dropped the bag. "Damn it, Red! I'm no expert on relationships but aren't we supposed to fight when we disagree? Couples do that."

He slowly stood. "I don't. Go put something on. Room service should be here any minute."

He infuriated her. "You want me to get dressed?"

"Yes."

She tore the towel off instead, balling it in her hands and throwing it at him. The damp towel hit him in the chest.

He appeared stunned for a split second before he glanced down her naked body. His gaze jerked up to hers. "What the hell are you doing?"

"I don't know," she admitted. "But yell at me. Something. Anything! This silent treatment is driving me crazy."

"Get dressed, Emma. They tend to bring food on a cart and push it into the room. I'll be damned if I let some human look at so much of you." He bent, picked up the towel, and tossed it back.

She caught it. "We're going to have words when I do." She snagged the bag and closed the bathroom door to investigate what Mandy had sent. There were no sleeping clothes but a T-shirt and sweats worked. Someone knocked on the door, and she wasted a little more time to avoid the hotel employee. The sound of the door closing and the bar being flipped was her que.

Red was at the table, transferring their food and drinks from the cart. She took a seat. "Want me to help?"

He dropped into the other seat. "Eat. Then we'll sleep."

"In separate beds, or are you going to share with me?"

He clenched his jaw.

So did she. He was so infuriating. "Is this our future? I do something that makes you mad and you giving me the cold shoulder? It sucks, Red. I can't do this. Talk to me. Yell at me. Something. We need to work it out."

He began to eat.

She wanted to stab him with the fork she unrolled from the cloth napkin, but instead she ate. It was the most uncomfortable meal she'd ever had in her life.

Red finished first then fled into the bathroom. The shower came on. Part of her was tempted to go after him. Let him try to ignore her if she stripped and climbed into the tiny space with him.

Reason won out. She finished eating and replaced everything on the cart, pushed it out of their room, and barred the door again. She picked the bed she figured Red would like best and pulled back the covers. She and her grandfather had stayed in many hotels. He always liked the bed nearest the door in case of attack. VampLycans were probably the same way.

She shoved off the sweats and got under the sheets. The shower shut off and forever seemed to pass before Red came out. The room went dark when Red flipped off the lights near the door, then she heard him moving—and the other bed creaking.

"Goddamn it!" she fumed. "You're not sleeping with me?"

Red said nothing.

"*Seriously*?"

"Get some sleep, Emma."

"Grandpa always told me to think things out before I said something when I was upset or angry, but you know what? I doubt he ever had to deal with someone as thick-headed and stubborn as you. Get your ass over here or I swear to God, once this is over, I won't return to Alaska. *Ever*. I refuse to become a mate to a guy who shuns me every time I do something he doesn't like."

Red startled her when his big body shoved hers flat on the bed. He had her pinned before she could even gasp. His hot, minty breath fanned her face, telling her he'd brushed his teeth in the bathroom while he'd been in there. She could barely make him out. The curtains over the window had to be blackout ones, since no light came through them from the street. She struggled to get her arms free of the sheets and reached out, finding his shoulders. His hair was wet, his skin a bit cold and still damp from the shower, and he wasn't wearing a shirt.

"You wanted me. Here I am," he growled. "Happy?"

She slid her hands to his back and clung to him, digging her fingers in but being careful of her nails. "No. I'm anything but. I'm sorry, Red. I know you don't want me in danger, but I have to try to save my grandpa." Tears filled her eyes. "I can't stand you treating me like this though."

His rigid body loosened a tiny bit and he sighed, adjusting his body over hers. "I'm so damn angry."

"I know."

"You've put me in hell."

"What do you mean?" She was glad he was talking to her. Even if he growled the words.

"I'll hate myself forever if anything happens to you. You expect me to just stand back while you enter that fucking house with a bunch of bloodsuckers. My instincts are screaming at me to protect you. But if I refuse to let you go, I lose you anyway, because you'll leave me even if you survive tomorrow. Who the fuck knows what they'll do? One of those bastards might want to breed you. I keep thinking it's better you're alive, even if you fucking hate me, than ever risk you dying. Then I think of life without you forever. I'm in fucking *hell*, Emma."

"I'm so sorry." She stroked his skin. "But I have to do this, Red."

He snarled and buried his face in her throat. His wet hair was cold, but she didn't care. He adjusted his body again, pinning her tighter against him by using both his arms and his weight. She wished the blankets weren't between them.

"I don't plan to die."

He opened his mouth, and his teeth gripped her throat in warning. She felt fangs and stilled. He wouldn't kill her, but she knew a bite would hurt.

He eased his grip and closed his mouth against her skin.

"You can't promise that," he finally said. "My father never meant to die either. He was an excellent fighter. I could give you a list of people I've lost in my life. Tough bastards, all of them killed. You're so fucking human. Fragile."

She stroked his back again. "They want me alive, Red."

"You don't know that for certain. We assume. For all we know, the council already killed Malachi and now they want you to show up there to wrap up any loose ends. That means *you*."

She hated to admit he could be right and silently let that horrible situation play out in her head. "Velder wants to send the council a message. He doesn't plan to kill those Vampires unless he has to. Only Eduardo is a guaranteed death."

"They're assassins for the council. Dying might be part of their job if it means taking out a target."

Again, she couldn't argue with him. It made sense. "I love you, Red. So much. I'd do anything for you…but I have to try to save my grandpa."

"I fucking know that." He lifted and rolled off her, sprawling on the bed beside her. He couldn't go far on the queen-size mattress.

She wiggled the covers out of the way and turned, snuggling up to him. He lifted his arm to let her get comfortable. She rested her head on his chest, listening to his rapidly beating heart. "Let's focus on what could go right instead. I go in there, Grandpa is rescued, and we're both fine. I'll introduce you to him and tell him we plan to be together for the rest of our lives."

He tightened his arm around her and pulled her closer. "Right. Then he'll go for my throat and try to kill me."

"He's not going to do that."

"You're his nest, Emma. *I'd* fucking kill to keep you. He will too."

"He'll want me happy."

"Then he shouldn't have left that damn message."

She winced at hearing him snarl, the vibrations that ran though his body when he did it. She caressed his stomach and ran her fingers lower. "No clothes? I'm shocked."

He gripped her wrist with his free hand and jerked her hand away from his cock. "No sex. You touch me like that and I'll fuck you. Then you'll be fucked tomorrow."

She frowned. "Why?"

He snarled again. "You should *know* why. No way are you prepared to go against Vampires."

Emma thought about it. "Scents. Never mind. I can shower you off if we just touch but the smell of sex tends to stay longer, especially if we don't use a condom. Got it. It would kill the surprise if they figure out I've been with a VampLycan."

He seemed to calm a little. "Yes. Mandy packed you clothes that were just washed and wore gloves to prevent her scent from getting on them. The bag is one she just purchased. She hadn't used it yet. It smells like plastic and the manufacturing company it came from. Remember to rub your shoes on the grass."

"I'm going to be okay, Red. I'm tough and smart."

"You're also frightened."

"Of course, I am. Who wouldn't be? I'm not a moron. Fear is a great thing. It keeps you sharp and a bit paranoid. I'll need both of those when I go inside the house."

He hugged her a little tighter. "I'll die if you do, Emma. You're my mate, even though you haven't let me claim you yet. How in the hell am I supposed to let you go when the time comes? How am I not supposed to lose my fucking mind and go in after you? That's why I've been quiet, and what you call sulking. I'm trying to keep a lid on this shit. Even now, my instincts are riding my ass to mate you. It would make you stronger, having my blood inside you. But it would also betray the plan, since they'd know you've been mated. They've been in the house you lived in for a little while now. They will have learned your scent well, since they don't know what you look like."

"Actually, they do." She went over every detail of when the Vampires had arrived and described the ones she'd seen. "Paula seemed to be in charge."

"I'm in hell! I just want to run off with you and lock you in my den."

"I'm going to be okay, Red. I have faith. Worst case, I fight. I'm not going in there without weapons. I just have to hold them off until you and the others come in after me. Just don't accidentally kill my grandpa, okay? Chances are, he's going to be the Vampire closest to me if he has an option. He'll put himself between me and the others."

"I won't kill him." He turned his head and brushed a kiss on the top of her head. "Don't die tomorrow."

"I won't. I promise." She hoped she could keep her word.

Chapter Twelve

Graves had come to their hotel room first thing the next morning. He'd stayed in the room, giving her advice, and kept sniffing near her to make sure no trace of VampLycan remained once she'd showered. He'd also brought a bag of clothes freshly purchased at the gift shop in the lobby. It had been slightly embarrassing to discover he'd included a bra and underwear. She hadn't asked him how he knew her sizes.

Red had sat in the chair across the room without saying a word. She met his grim gaze often but didn't try to provoke him into talking. It was easier to deal with the silent treatment after he'd explained it was the only way he could keep control of his instincts and emotions.

At the end, when she was ready to leave the room and he stood, the desire to hug him almost overwhelmed her.

"You can't," Graves stated softly. "I'm sorry."

She glanced at him.

"I don't have a mate, but I know I'd want to hold her if she was walking out the door into uncertainty. You'd have to take another shower, I'd need to buy you more clothes, and we're on a time constraint. We must go. The rental car we arranged has been dropped off." He flashed his phone. "My brother accepted the keys but didn't get inside. I doubt the Vamps will come out to sniff the car since they'd get burned unless you parked in the garage, which isn't in the plan. But just in case, it smells all human right now. Better to be safe than sorry. For all we know, they could have hired a rogue Were for this job. He could sniff the car for them."

Her gaze returned to Red. "I've got this. I know you're coming for me once I'm inside. I love you. We'll tell Grandpa about us and tonight, you can bite me."

He looked positively tortured as he gave a sharp nod.

She sucked in a sharp breath and opened the door, stepping out into the hallway. Graves was careful not to touch her. They took the same elevator down to the lobby. He led her to the parking structure and she spotted Micah. No one else from their group was in sight.

"You drive the route discussed. No variations." Graves glanced at his phone again. "Don't break the speed limit either. We'll get there right after you but watch the fucking time. Slow down if you're too early. You hit that driveway right at noon. Not before."

Micah chuckled. "I checked the dash clock. It's twenty-one seconds faster than my phone." He tossed her a key fob.

She caught it, noticing he wore gloves. "Thanks."

"I put a surprise in the trunk. That's why I had my brother buy you a baggy sweatshirt." He tapped his inner forearm. "Straps on right here. You grip the sides of it near your elbow with both your finger and thumb, push the buttons at the same time, and a six-inch blade slides down. Make sure you curl your hand back and don't accidently stab yourself. The spring on it is fast, and it's sharp enough to do damage. Go for their throats and eye sockets if you need to use it." He glanced at her, up and down. "You look utterly human." He sniffed. "Smell like one, too. I hope to hell you've got some surprises of your own."

"I'm faster than a human, and stronger. I'd put you on your ass to show you but we're being careful of how I smell. You'd win in a fight once you drew your claws, but I'd give you a run for your money at first."

He smiled. "I'm glad to hear it." It was gone fast. "Go in slow. Act unafraid to enter the house."

"No problem." She *was* afraid, but the Vampires wouldn't be able to smell that unless they were close.

"Be loud once you're inside. Raise hell but don't give them a reason to hurt you," Graves advised. "Try to avoid them touching you. Velder wants some of them alive and your mate is seriously on edge. He'll probably rip apart any who carried your scent."

Micah stepped aside. "Get in the car, adjust the seat, and take your time. Everyone is meeting us at the van. We'll get to the property a few minutes after you. I put a tracker on the car just to be certain of your location at all times."

She fisted the key. "Got it." She stared at him for a moment. "You look tired."

"I didn't sleep. I shifted instead and did some scouting. It would have screwed up everything if we couldn't find the tunnel entrance. It hasn't been disturbed. The Vamps haven't discovered it, or I'd have noticed that it had been opened recently. I'm leading everyone there. It was well hidden. Good job."

"Grandpa did that. I only helped him dig it out."

"I just hope it's not too fucking tight."

"It's not. Grandpa isn't a small Vampire. He has some muscle to him and he's tall. He fits fine."

Graves got her attention. "Watch for anyone coming at you the closer you get to the house. We'll be a few miles behind you. As I said, they might have hired rogue Weres. It's paramount that you reach that house and not be taken to another location. Micah couldn't risk getting too close to the house while scouting but he saw lights. It would be a fucking nightmare if they've switched homes and tried to grab you on the way."

"In other words," Micah added. "Turn this vehicle into a weapon if you have to. Don't get kidnapped." He nodded and left, heading for the van.

"As you said, you've got this." Graves hesitated. "I deal with a lot of unstable situations, considering what I do. Just try to stay calm and use your head. Don't panic even if it seems like everything is going to hell. You have the advantage no matter what, because you know we're going to show up. They don't."

"Thanks."

He left too, and she approached the rental. It was something she wouldn't have chosen. A four-door sedan in a light brown. It looked like something a conservative family would pick. She got in, adjusted the seat and mirrors, and put on her belt. The engine came to life without problems when she inserted and twisted the key.

She knew the area well, since they were in the larger town near where the house was located. She'd steered toward its lights the night she'd gone off the roof. It would be a twenty-minute drive, and the tank was full.

"I can do this," she whispered, putting the car in reverse to back out of the parking space. "I'm coming, Grandpa." He'd be pissed at her, but at least he'd be alive. Her grip on the steering wheel tightened.

Traffic wasn't bad once she left the city. It was part of the reason they had moved farther away and up into the mountain. The roads were curvy as she made her way up a back on they'd chosen. It wasn't her normal route. Her gaze kept going to the trees and heavily wooded areas as the homes thinned. It would be the perfect place for a Lycan rogue to run out into the road.

"I'll run you over. Not stopping. Not getting kidnapped," she muttered. "Your ass will be roadkill, only I doubt you'd die. You'd just want to."

She glanced at the clock and slowed down a little. No traffic was behind her but on a curve, she quickly glanced down the mountain and saw the top of the commercial van. Red and the others were following. She finally came to the turn that would take her to the house, and knew they'd go straight. She hit the brakes at the stop sign and said a little prayer.

"Hey, Mom. Don't be mad at me, please. I know you lost your life saving mine. You can't blame me for risking mine today. Watch out for me and Grandpa. We could use a little guardian angel help about now."

She took her foot off the brake and glanced at the clock. She turned right and, down the road, slowed again, watching for the driveway. Grandpa had thought about installing a gate but hadn't. He considered intruders surprise snacks if anyone ever showed up to rob them. So far, no one had ever tried to break in.

That made her smile. Grandpa's sense of humor always cracked her up. She glanced at the clock again as she spotted the gap in the trees and paved road. "Here we go. I'm on time. Well, a minute early, but I'll drive slow."

She turned and crawled up the narrow road. The house came into view and she hit the brakes again. It was a beautiful day, the sun shining and not even a little overcast. That was a good thing. Nothing rushed at her on four or two legs. That was an even better thing. Maybe the Vampire Council didn't like working with rogue Lycans. She was fine with that. What waited inside the house would be bad enough.

The clock on the dash hit noon and she drove slowly forward and parked in the circular driveway. About thirty feet separated the car from the front door.

She took some deep breaths, masked her features in case they had figured out how to access the security cameras on the outside of the house, and climbed out of the car. She stretched, her gaze darting toward the woods around her. They kept it mostly cleared in the front. No movement. *So far, so good.* She closed the door and strolled to the trunk as if she didn't have a care in the world.

The fob had a button for the trunk. She hit it and the trunk popped open, revealing a bag, and next to it lie a metal weapon with Velcro. She mentally went over where the cameras were and stepped closer, blocking the view. It took her only a few seconds to see it was a thin, narrow blade in a holder, one side revealing the sharp tip and the other solid. Two buttons rested along the sides near the hilt. She shoved up her sleeve as she leaned in, quickly putting it on. The baggy sweatshirt hid it as she yanked the sleeve down to her wrist. She grabbed the bag and slammed the lid closed.

The van should have reached where they planned to park. The only unknown was how long it would take them to crawl through that tunnel one at a time. It wasn't as if they could test it out beforehand. She walked around the car to the front passenger side and bent, as if examining the front wheel. Later, she'd apologize to Red for what she was about to do. She'd implied she was going in armed. Vampires would smell guns.

She rose up and stretched again, trying to appear as if she'd just driven a long way. She even stopped a few times on her way to the front door and did some knee bends and rubbed the middle of her back. She'd have aches if she'd just spent a lot of time behind a wheel.

To waste more time, she took a little stroll to the grass, rubbed her shoes the way she'd been told, and picked up a stick, tossing it into the bushes. It was time to go in.

She left the grassy area and got back on the walkway to the front porch.

She focused her mind hard on her grandpa. *"Grandpa? Can you hear me?"*

There was no answer inside her head.

"Grandpa, please answer me."

It scared her when he didn't respond. He would have if he could. Was he sleeping or had they hurt him? She needed to get inside.

She stopped at the alarm box and shut it down before she had the system unlock the doors. Not just the front, but all of them. She also took a moment to reset the code to a new one. That way the Vampires couldn't turn it back on. She forced a yawn as she worked quickly. There was a camera looking down on her from above, but the lens couldn't see the pad or anything she entered.

No one jerked open the door as she reached for it, though she was half expecting that. It turned in her hand and she walked in.

Her gaze took in the living room and stairs. No one waited to grab her. She closed the door, pretended to lock it by doing a half turn of the lock, then turning it back. The bag, she dropped at her feet, then she turned to glance at the stairs and entryway to the kitchen.

"Honey, I'm home!" she yelled. "Yo, sleepy head. I drove all night. The least you could do is get your old ass up and greet me!"

Movement from above came from the corner of her eye. She jerked her head up right as Paula dropped from one of the beams that ran the length of the living room. She had to have been lying in wait.

"Fuck!" Emma didn't mean to, but she stumbled backward in surprise and slammed her head against the door. It didn't hurt but she stayed still.

Another Vamp came from the kitchen. Two more stepped out of her grandpa's office to her left. She looked up, seeing three more at the top of the stairs.

Her gaze returned to Paula. It wasn't hard to fake fear. She felt the real thing.

"Hello, Emma."

"Fuck," she repeated. "Where's Malachi?" She purposely used his name.

"He's tied up at the moment." The Vamp strolled closer, the color of her eyes getting brighter.

Emma lowered her gaze to her lips to avoid being mind-controlled. "What's going on? He said you left." She hoped her acting was up to par as she crossed her arms protectively over her stomach, hoping to hide the weapon strapped to her inner arm, more than worrying the assassin would gut her. "Oh shit…you tricked me."

"It was easy to do." Paula came closer and sniffed her. "Human…" She quickly backed up. "I don't understand. Eduardo!"

Emma flinched as the woman bellowed.

Paula hauled her away from the door. "You run, and I kill Malachi. Understand? Don't try to flee outside." The Vamp shoved Emma into the living room but let her go.

Her worst nightmare came out of her grandpa's office. "How are you awake during the day?"

The years hadn't done Eduardo's memory justice. She'd forgotten more than she thought she had. He could have passed her on the street and she wouldn't have given him more than a wary glance. He looked younger than she remembered, maybe nineteen, almost boyish. He wasn't tall or solidly built, either. He stood at maybe five feet six, perhaps weighing in around one thirty. His hair had been cut close to his head. Her four-year-old memory had him looking way meaner and bigger than the reality.

Then their gazes met, and she was sure it was him by the pure hatred he directed at her.

He sneered at her. "I drank blood from friends." Eduardo tore his attention to Paula. "Why are you mad? We have her. I told you she'd come."

"You also said she was VampLycan. She doesn't smell like it." Paula lunged, moving fast and grabbing him. She lifted him a few inches off his feet and flashed fang, hissing. "This is the human who warms his bed. I met her when we first arrived."

Eduardo struggled until the woman dropped him, and then glowered at Emma. "She looks exactly like that malamute bitch Mal sired. She's his kin. I don't care what she smells like."

Paula turned to Emma, studying her intently. "Are you VampLycan?"

Red and the group should have reached the tunnels. She hoped so, anyway. It was time to keep the Vamps' attention. "I'm not answering shit until I get to see Malachi." Then she glared at Eduardo and started to yell. "Did you kill him? You're such an asshole. Do the world a favor and go find some cow's tit to suck on, you sniveling baby! Oh, poor you, your master left you. Who the fuck wouldn't? I know all about you. You turned on him after he saved your life. You're nothing but a fucking *pussy!*"

He roared in rage and flew at her. The other Vampires rushed forward, two of them grabbing him.

They weren't allowing him to get to her. It encouraged Emma.

"You call Kallie a malamute bitch? Ha! You're a *traitor*. And did you tell the council how you risked exposing Vampires by killing at least twenty humans in that community you butchered? I bet you didn't.

Because they'd kill your stupid ass instead of helping you track a master who doesn't want you! You're fucking pathet—"

An open hand slamming against her chest had Emma flying backward, and she landed the couch. It hurt. She rolled through the pain and jumped over the couch, grabbing the first thing her hand could reach. It was a statue of a horse. She'd bought it in Spain.

It could be replaced.

She threw it at Paula's head, since she was the one who'd hit her.

"What?" She kept yelling, grabbing another statue. "You don't want everyone to hear what Eduardo did in the past? There are rules Vampires must follow. That asshole broke them. Why are you even here instead of ashing his ass?" She chucked the statue at a male Vampire who'd taken a step toward her, and then dashed to the fireplace. Neither of the statues had hit their targets, but they made lots of noise as they smashed on the floors, breaking when the Vamps dodged them.

She grabbed the fire poker and shovel, waving them. It wasn't an accident when she hit a few things on the mantel and they came crashing down next to her. She glared at Paula. "You want to know what I am? Where the fuck is Malachi? Answer me and I'll tell you."

Paula's eyes brightened and Emma threw the poker at her. The Vamp slid a few inches over and it slammed into the glass table behind her, shattering it.

Emma yelled again. "Malachi? Where are you?"

"Enough!" Paula stormed closer.

Emma chucked the shovel, hitting the mirror over the fireplace. It shattered. She used every ounce of speed she had to avoid the enraged Vamp and threw her body out of the way. She hit the floor hard, rolled under the long side table they used to separate part of the living room from the walkway to the kitchen, and came up on the other side. It wouldn't stop a Vamp but the bitch would have to jump over it.

Emma made it to the kitchen hallway and grabbed the glass cabinet that stored some china. She slid her fingers behind the heavy piece of furniture and shoved with all her strength. It crashed over, almost landing on top of Paula. She ran into the kitchen to the pantry, tore open the door, and grabbed one of her grandfather's swords. No one had moved it. The Vamps probably hadn't searched where human food was stored.

She turned right as three Vamps entered, Paula leading the charge. Emma leapt up, landing on the island, and crouched slightly, sword held in front of her. "Where the fuck is Malachi? If you killed him, I'll take your damn heads."

Paula looked shocked. "You're *not* human."

"No shit, bitch. What did you do with my master?"

"You aren't a Vampire, either."

"Two for two," Emma yelled. "Is he alive?" She rose up as more Vampires entered the kitchen after they'd dragged the broken cabinet out of the hallway. Seven of them stared up at her on the island. "Answer me, damn it. *Where is he?* What have you done with him?"

Eduardo came into the kitchen, stomping on the broken glass. "I told you she was VampLycan. I didn't lie."

"You lie about *everything*, asshole." Emma tightened both hands on the hilt of the sword. "Why don't you come at me now, you coward? I'll tell you where another sword is to even the fight. I want to fucking kill you so bad. *You murdered my mother!* I'll take your fucking head! I'd shove it up your own ass but you'd ash too fast."

Two more Vampires came in. Emma silently wondered how many others there were, and if her grandpa was even alive. If he wasn't, they'd all die. She didn't care what Velder wanted. They'd pay for killing him.

For now, she had their attention. That's all that mattered at the moment.

She jumped off the island, away from them, and swung her blade, taking out everything on the counter. More glass shattered and the coffee maker broke apart. "Did you kill him?"

"Put down the sword. We're not going to kill you," Paula hissed. "I'm from the council, and that's a fucking *order*, Emma."

"They aren't *my* council." She swung the sword again, this time taking out the mugs that hung from the cute hooks she'd bought on the internet. It was a good thing she knew they'd never stay in the house again. The mess she was making would take forever to clean. "Where. Is. Mal?"

"He's fine. Just contained," Paula took a step closer. "Put down that sword." Her eyes lit up.

Emma dropped her gaze to her lip. "Guess what? Your voice doesn't do shit for me and I'm not stupid enough to let you look into my eyes. Fuck you. I want to see him. Where is he? I'm not telling you shit or doing anything you want unless you can prove he's alive."

"He's in his office."

"In the safe, to be precise," Eduardo snickered.

Horror hit—and Emma lost her shit. "The tiny one in the wall? *You ashed him?*"

She screamed and lunged for Eduardo.

He tried to dodge but he didn't seem to understand she could move faster than he expected. Part of the blade sliced his arm and he roared. Three of the Vamps jumped toward her and the sword was torn from her hands. She hit the wall hard enough that part of it gave way. Drywall dug into her skin. She screamed and fought.

They didn't expect that and tried to get a better hold on her. She collapsed her legs and ended up on her ass. It loosened their holds and she twisted, rolling into their legs, and went for the blade Micah hand given her. She remembered to twist her wrist back in time to prevent the blade from impaling her palm.

She shoved it upward, nailing one of the bastards in the groin. His scream was piercing.

The kitchen wasn't a big space with the massive island. She stayed down on the floor, slashing at them as they tried to grab her, and more came forward to help. They tripped over each other, going down. She braced against the floor for traction and leapt up, landing on the island, and was tackled from the side.

"Don't kill her!" Paula shouted.

That answered that. Not that Emma had time to care, as she was slammed hard into the floor with some asshole on top of her. He pinned the arm with the weapon beside her head.

She avoided his eyes, the pain, and used her free hand to grab his crotch. *Squeeze hard and twist.*

He shrieked in pain and let go of her arm with the blade to try to remove her hand from his nuts. It was a mistake, and she rammed the blade into his throat. He threw his body off her. She scrambled away, into the corner, and stood up.

More Vamps came at her, until she was pinned like a bug to the wall. They held her arms out to her sides. Her body felt crushed, there were so many hands.

Paula shoved her way in close enough to grab her chin.

"Look at me."

Emma squeezed her eyes closed. "Fuck you!"

A roar tore through the kitchen...and then all hell *really* broke loose.

Something smashed through the window nearest her, and Emma was able to turn her head when Paula released her jaw. She opened her eyes, seeing the shade was torn off and a body-size hole now gaped where the glass used to be. Someone screamed. Probably the Vamp who was thrown out the hole and was now burning in the sun.

There was a twenty-something-foot drop on that side to the walkout basement area, and no shade.

The cavalry had arrived. Vamps let her go as they turned to fight but were grabbed and pinned instead by enraged VampLycans.

Red got to her first. He lifted her, hugging her so tight she felt pretty sure he cracked some ribs, if they weren't already in that condition. She burst into sobs.

"I've got you, baby. Where are you hurt? What did those bastards do to you?"

She remembered the blade and tried hard not to stab him as she clung to him. "They killed Grandpa!"

"God. It's going to be okay, baby. I've got you."

Her sobs grew worse. She was safe…but she hadn't been able to rescue her grandpa.

Chapter Thirteen

The Vampires were subdued. There were fourteen in all. It seemed Graves had brought industrial handcuffs and some spiked chains. They were trussed up and shoved on their knees. The rescue team had dragged all of them inside the living room and had shoved back the furniture to keep them all together.

Emma sipped the water that Red had made her drink. She had cried while they'd cleared the house and captured every Vampire trapped inside. It wasn't as if the Vamps could run outside into the sunshine. Graves and Micah had protected the tunnel once they'd entered the house. No one had gotten past them.

She glared at Eduardo.

"He's mine." She locked gazes with Velder. "I get his head. He killed my mother. But they *all* die since they murdered my grandpa. None of them get to live. Do what you must, then it's my right to ash these bastards."

"Master Malachi is not dead," Paula stated clearly. She tried to stand.

Lake shoved her back on her ass. "Stay down," he snarled.

Emma pulled out of Red's hold. "Where did you take him then? The house was searched, and *that* asshat," she pointed at Eduardo, "said you put Grandpa in his office safe. It's twelve inches by ten inches."

"We found one upstairs in a walk-in closet, carried it downstairs, and crammed him inside." Paula sighed. "The master will be fine once he's given some blood. He was too difficult to control. We had to put him to sleep."

"Oh my God!" Emma was glad Red stayed close as her knees almost buckled. He caught her and held her against his front. "You assholes suffocated him? When? How long has he been in there?" She tried to wiggle out of Red's hold to rush to find her grandpa but he tightened his arms around her.

"Not yet," he whispered. "We'll get him."

Paula directed her attention to Velder. "You seem to be the one in charge. I'm here on behalf of the Vampire Council. Master Malachi and his granddaughter have been accused of crimes. We're here to capture and bring them both in to be tried."

"That's a lie. Who said we broke laws? The asshat?" Emma wanted to wring Eduardo's neck and then rip it off his body. "He's a liar."

Velder growled low and shook his head at her. "Silence, Emma. Let's hear what they have to say. I'm more than curious." He faced her and grinned. It was gone in an instant when he turned to face the Vamps. "Your name?"

"Paula. These are my nest members you hold captive."

"Including Eduardo? Did he join your little assassin team?"

Surprise showed on Paula's face, but she recovered fast. "No."

"I'm aware of what you do for your council, and your *teams* are not part of any nest." Velder took a seat on a chair and got comfortable. "What's the real reason you came after them, Paula? Don't play games with me. Your lives are in my hands."

Paula lowered her head and tried to look submissive. Emma didn't buy it, judging from her tense body. She would bet the Vampire inwardly seethed and hid her eyes to hide her real emotions.

"Master Malachi abandoned his nest and left them in chaos. That is against our laws. He chose this Emma over his nest as well. Blood is first and foremost. She's not his child."

"I see. Emma *is* his blood though, isn't she? She did come first. What's *her* crime, according to your council?"

"He abandoned his nest and harbored a child that shouldn't have been born." Her head lifted, her face an emotionless mask. "It's against your own laws for VampLycans to breed without permission." A cold smile formed on her lips. "We were trying to contain the situation and honor you by arresting her. The council would have contacted you to let you know of her existence."

Velder threw back his head and laughed. "I bet they would have."

Paula's smile faded and her eyes narrowed.

Velder stopped laughing and leaned forward, putting his hands on his thighs. When he spoke, his voice held anger. "That's a good one."

"I don't understand."

"I love your explanation. You mean they would have used her for leverage in some way against us if you'd been able to bring Emma to them. Kallie, Emma's mother, was a part of my clan." He stood. "Let me introduce myself. I'm Velder, clan leader." He took a threatening step toward Paula. "My clan does *not* need permission to breed. It's you Vampires who aren't allowed to touch a Lycan without approval, since you can't be trusted to ensure it's consensual. Emma is one of mine...and you've admitted to coming after her. Is the council declaring war on VampLycans?"

Glacier stepped forward. "That would mean the GarLycans as well." Glacier nodded at another man who resembled him. She figured it must be his brother, since it was the first time she'd seen him. "We back the VampLycans on all things. You take on clan, you get both."

Their skin began to change color and Emma sealed her mouth tight. Both brothers turned their skin into a kind of gray armor. It was cool but scary-looking too. Her attention went to Paula to see her reaction.

Paula's already pale face whitened even more. She shook her head. "The council doesn't want a war. We thought we were doing you a service. Clans live together. Emma seemed rogue to us. We were certain the VampLycans weren't aware of her existence."

"You and they were wrong." Velder motioned the GarLycan brothers back. "War is what they almost started by sending you here. You tell your council Emma belongs to *us*. As for Malachi, he might be a Vampire, but he's considered mine too."

"You have no right!"

Velder snarled. "I have no right? I'm half Vampire. You're telling me we can't claim family ties to our sires?" He let his claws slide out of his fingertips. "We *exist* because Vampires wanted to breed. Well, take a good look."

One of the VampLycans removed his clothes and shifted until he stood on four legs. He growled at the Vampires and let them get an up-close look at his body. Emma glanced at the Vamps—they appeared terrified.

"Bet if they could piss, they would right now," she whispered.

Velder shot her a dirty look. She decided not to make any more comments. Red brushed a kiss on the top of her head.

"I think they get the point." Velder nodded at the beasty man. "Thank you, Jarred. You can put your clothes back on." He walked over to Paula and crouched, leaving only a few feet between them. "Do you want to pick a team member to take on one of my VampLycans to see if you fight better than we do? You'd watch one of yours get ashed. We don't fuck around. Malachi *is* one of mine. He fathered VampLycans, and unlike most of your kind, he didn't *force* the Lycan who birthed his children. He's clan. VampLycan's don't need permission to breed. Emma is the child of one. You have no right to attempt to capture any of our kind. You tell that to your damn council."

Paula dropped her head. "We were just trying to offer justice for the past. I was unaware of the willingness of his breeder. But Master Malachi still abandoned his nest. He shouldn't have formed one if he didn't plan to rule them. My council wants him to be tried for that."

Emma felt frustrated. It was bullshit. She wanted to say as much but Red tightened his hold. She looked up at him and he gave her a slight shake of his head. "Trust us," he mouthed. She did. She said nothing.

Velder lowered his hand to the floor, claws out, and braced it inches from where Paula sat. "You mean the nest that disregarded Malachi's orders and killed four of my VampLycans? Four of my clan? *That* nest?" The words were said with deadly calm and a chilling tone. "The same nest who tried to murder a child of my clan, forcing Malachi to flee to spare her from being slaughtered? That fucking nest?"

Paula curled into her body and lowered her head more. "That's not what we were told."

Glacier's brother snorted. "Again? It's like your number-one excuse. Some bloodsucker lies, and you don't bother to check it out first before sending assassins after the wrong person? Fucking morons."

Velder snapped his head toward the man. "Tempest, I've got this."

The GarLycan threw up his hands. "Sorry. My bad. It's just frustrating. I'm volunteering though if you want me to demonstrate the GarLycan blender move. My wings can rip through Vampires like a blade through wet tissue paper. I get fucking testy when they do this shit. Learn, dipshits."

Velder chuckled. "I understand, but no demonstration needed."

"See why we call him Pest?" Glacier muttered.

Velder rose to his feet. "Paula, you and your fellow assassins are ordered to stay put. I'll listen if you wish to live. It's not as if you have anywhere to go. I hope for your sake Malachi is whole and can be revived. Your lives depend on it." He backed up. "Except for Eduardo."

The shithead whimpered.

"He's ours." Paula lifted her head.

"Emma, come forward."

Red released her. She walked up to Velder's side. He reached out to place a hand on her shoulder and stopped her from getting any closer to the Vampires. "Can you identify the one who attacked you as a child? The one who murdered your mother and our other VampLycans?"

She was more than happy to point Eduardo out, and did. "That asshole."

"You fucking *bitch*," Eduardo hissed. "Your mother cried while we bled her! She tasted like shit!"

Emma was filled with rage and tried to go after him. Velder hooked his arm around her waist and pushed her back. Red's arms embraced her from behind and he lifted her off her feet. Velder gripped her face with both of his hands. She stilled as he leaned in, holding her gaze.

"His life is yours to take. Let's get Malachi first and see how painful you get to make it. Justice is yours."

Tears blinded her, and she nodded.

Velder backed away and glanced at the men with him. "GarLycans, if you'd please keep the assassin team and the murderer company, I would appreciate it. Tempest, if they try to attack, show them your blender move. Just wait for me to return before you do. I admit I'm morbidly curious."

Red put Emma on her feet and released her and she rushed toward her grandpa's office. It had been trashed. All the books on the shelves lay on the floor as if the Vampires were looking for something. Some of the furniture had been broken and smashed. Blood stained the carpet in places. It looked like one hell of a fight had happened, and she knew her grandpa had been involved.

The large safe sat in one corner, stained with dried blood. She ran forward and dropped on her knees, trying to calm her mind enough to remember the combination.

"Do you know it?" Red crouched next to her.

"Yes. Grandpa keeps our papers and some of my childhood art projects in it." Tears blinded her, and she wiped them away. She had to use her fingernail to scratch some of the crusted blood off the dial to read the numbers. It was a mistake to inhale through her nose.

"It's Grandpa's blood." It tore her up, knowing he must have suffered. It wasn't a big safe. He had to be balled up tight to fit. He'd have suffocated fast, trapped, and lost consciousness, his body starved for air.

The lock clicked, and she yanked the heavy door open.

A moan tore from her at the sight.

He was in there, his clothing covered with dried blood, and the skin that she could see had turned a dark color it shouldn't have been—a ghastly shade of grayish blue. The stench of decayed blood made her gag.

Red grabbed her around the waist and hauled them both to their feet. He backed up, and she watched as Velder and two other VampLycans crowded down to get her grandpa out.

"Fuck," Lake muttered. "His body isn't showing signs of rigor mortis but all the blood on his jeans and sweater is stiff as hell."

"Be careful with his neck," Velder whispered. "They really packed him in. Jarred, try to move him down a little to get his head clear."

Emma bit her lip, grateful that they were getting her grandpa out. "He needs blood."

"Not yours."

She stared up at Red. "I'm his granddaughter."

"And you're fucking tiny. I'll offer up a vein."

She didn't care who fed her grandpa, as long as he woke okay. The men inched back and put her grandpa on the floor in front of the safe. His clothing made sickening sounds as they attempted to straighten his body to lay him flat on his back. She tried to get closer but Red wouldn't allow it.

He held her tighter. "Stay here with me. They'll help him."

Emma struggled but Red was too strong. "I need to do this! Grandpa's out of it. The smell of fresh blood should bring down his fangs. I'm supposed to place a bag of it over his mouth."

Velder turned his head and held her gaze. "How much blood will he need to fully recover?"

"I don't know. This has never happened. We just talked about it. He said to get a pint of blood, that would rouse him, and it should be enough to clear his head to make sure that he's not mindless. We figured he could hunt for a donor after that."

"What does he normally consume? How much?"

"A few pints a week in all. He doesn't have to feed nightly. That's only when he's not so injured though." Her gaze went to her grandpa's face—she instantly regretted it. Her grandpa looked dead and horrible. Nothing like his normal self. His blond hair appeared even starker white compared to his now dark skin.

Velder sighed, bending over her grandpa and blocking her view. "It will be fine. All the VampLycans will offer up blood. Except you, Emma. You're already injured."

Graves came forward. "A pint from each of you three should be enough. If not, I'll offer my blood too."

Emma nodded. "Three pints healed him after he got shot seven times."

Everyone turned to stare at her.

"What?"

"Who shot him seven times? And *why*?"

She looked up at Red. "I told you my grandpa likes to play hero. There was a drive-by shooting while he was talking a walk. He tackled the humans in harm's way and took the bullets instead."

"He's a fucking saint." Red sighed and rolled his eyes.

Emma lightly punched him. "For the last time, he's not bad."

"I get it. Let's hope he doesn't want to kill me when we tell him you're my mate."

"Emma?" Velder turned. "His fangs aren't down."

"Cut a finger and rub some blood under his nose. It should work."

Velder bent over her grandfather once more. "It did. They slid down. Now what? Just shove my arm on his fangs?"

"And try to hit a vein."

"Got it." Velder paused and then hissed. "That hurt. Fangs are in. He's not moving."

Emma had been schooled well by her grandpa. "Give it a minute. His fangs will automatically draw blood and once it hits his system, be careful. He might come up fighting."

More VampLycans came forward and crouched, ready to pounce if needed.

Emma tried to go closer but Red continued to hold her back. "They won't hurt him. We know what starved or severely injured Vamps are like. Trust us, Emma."

They were clan. She needed to get used to that concept. It was hard though and would take a while.

"I know it's just been the two of you, but not anymore," Red rasped next to her ear.

Grandpa's leg jerked and a low growl came from him.

"Hold him down," Velder demanded. "Malachi, look at me." He deepened his voice. "It's Velder. Stop fighting. That's my arm in your mouth. Drink, old friend. VampLycans are holding you. It's safe. We've got you."

Emma couldn't see her grandpa with so many big bodies in the way. Her grandpa's leg stopped moving and he went still.

"That's it." Velder's tone softened. "The Vampires who did this to you are restrained and contained. Emma is here and safe. Just drink. No, you can take more. I'm not feeling light-headed."

"I don't want to weaken you."

Emma felt tears sliding down her face at hearing her grandpa's voice, even if it sounded weak and hoarse.

"Take as much as you need from us. This is Lake. Bite his arm. You look like shit, Malachi. We've got plenty of donors willing to get you back to your old self." Velder turned his head and smiled at Emma, nodding. "He's all intact. Got all his fingers and toes."

Jarred chuckled. "He kind of looks like a shelled Gargoyle, only with some blue."

"His fangs work fine, Emma." Lake moved a little to smile at her. "He's drinking like a champ."

Velder stood. "Red, why don't you take Emma out of here. Maybe for a walk outside. I wouldn't want my granddaughter to see me in this condition. We'll get him a shower after he's fed enough to completely heal."

"I want to stay," Emma protested.

Velder met her gaze. "Not a request."

Red pulled her out of the office. She didn't fight, going with him willingly. He led her out the front door and into the sunshine. "Malachi will be fine. Men have pride, Emma. Let Malachi get cleaned up and then you can talk to him."

She turned and threw her arms around his waist. "Just hold me."

"Forever." He hugged her tight. "You're hurt. Don't think I've forgotten about that. I can smell your blood. How bad is it? I've been damn patient since you haven't fainted or complained of being in pain."

"I'm not sure," she admitted. "Nothing too serious. A lot of bruising, some cuts, and maybe a few cracked ribs. I'll heal fast."

He growled, gentling his hold. "You should drink some of my blood."

"I'll wait until we officially mate. I'm good."

"You need a shower. Those Vampires were touching you."

"My room is upstairs. I have a private bathroom."

"Let's go."

"Velder said to stay outside."

"My uncle can get over it once I tell him why we went inside. I want to check you over myself and see if any of those fuckers need to die. Are you sure you're not seriously hurt?"

"I've had worse than this in training. The Vampires were attempting to capture me. Not hurt me."

He snarled.

She just smiled and promised, "I'm fine, Red."

"You'd better be."

He turned, staring at the house. "Is there another way in? I don't even want you near those bastards."

"We could go in at the side of the house and use the back stairs near the mudroom."

"Show me."

She let her arms drop. Red grabbed her hand, lacing their fingers together. She smiled, walking around the house. Her gaze lifted to the clear blue sky. *Thanks for looking out for us, Mom.*

Chapter Fourteen

Red hated everything about the house. Emma had said it was big. His cabin could have fit inside it and there would still be a good fifteen thousand square feet. It was a huge mansion. Her bedroom alone was bigger than his living room and kitchen combined, and her bathroom beat the size of his bedroom. Not only did it have a huge jacuzzi tub, but a shower they could have thrown a party inside.

All of it depressed him. How could she possibly give all this up to be happy with him in Alaska?

He watched her shower through the clear glass, documenting every bruise, cut, and scrape on her skin. He wanted to go beat on some Vampires downstairs for doing that to her. She shut off the three showerheads and pushed open the glass door. He grabbed a towel, opened it, and began to dry her.

She smiled. "I'm fine, Red. You're treating me like I'm a baby."

"You're *my* baby."

She chuckled. "That's kind of hot and disturbing at the same time. I'm never calling you Daddy."

He snorted. "I hope not. That's something I'm not into." He backed away when she wrapped the towel around herself and passed her another. "For your hair."

"Thank you."

"You have double sinks and a vanity."

She glanced around. "It's horrible, isn't it?"

He scowled. "It's the nicest bathroom I've ever seen."

"Sing. I bet it echoes in here. Whoever built this house either liked to waste a lot of space or thought they should be an opera singer. I've never used that vanity. I don't even wear makeup. Grandpa bitches about the smell and tells me only working women wear it.—that's his kind way to say 'hooker.' Then again, way back when, that was probably true. When I was a kid, I once asked him if he rode any dinosaurs when he was my age."

Red was amused. "I bet you gave him hell."

"All the time."

He followed her out of the bathroom to her walk-in closet. It was mostly empty. "You don't have many clothes."

She snickered. "You mean because I only use this tiny section? Twenty people could share this closet." She pulled a pair of leggings off a hanger and then grabbed an oversized black shirt. "Do me a favor?"

"Anything."

"Why don't you start shoving my clothes into the two suitcases in that corner? I might as well take it all when we leave."

He didn't move.

She turned to him, staring. "What? You don't want to pack for me? No problem. It won't take me long to do it."

"Are you still coming to Alaska with me?"

She stepped closer. "Did you change your mind about us being mates?"

"Fuck no, but how can I compare with this?" He waved his arms.

"I hate this monstrosity of a house, Red." She dropped her clothes and pressed up against him, putting her hands on his chest. "Those aren't just words to make you feel better. Grandpa got this place cheap. No one else wanted to take it on. And whatever you do, don't open any of the other doors up here. There's got to be an inch of dust layered on every surface. No way was I cleaning spaces we didn't use. I *love* your cabin. It's cozy and comfortable. Have you once thought of either of those descriptions since you've been in this house?"

"No." He gripped her hips. "You didn't mention loving my den." He smiled.

"That's going to take some adjusting. Big metal box buried in the ground. For you though, I'll be motivated to love it." She stroked him with her hands. "Are you going to pack my stuff or am I? Face it…I'm yours."

He loved hearing that from her. "What if Malachi forbids you to be with me?" It was his worst fear.

"He won't, Red."

"What if he does?"

She licked her lips. "I love my grandpa. I owe him my life." She rose up on her tiptoes, holding his gaze with hers. "You're my future, Red. I love you too. I can't see him being upset but if he is, he'll get over it with time. I'm going home with you to Alaska."

He grinned. "Good. It's where you belong."

"Anywhere you are."

He lowered his head and kissed her. He kept it light though. They needed to return downstairs to speak to Malachi, and he was curious what his Uncle Velder would do with the Vampire assassins. Then he remembered Eduardo as he pulled away from her soft, tempting lips.

"I'll kill Eduardo for you."

She dropped on her heels. "He's mine."

He reached up and cupped her face. "You shouldn't have to live with death, Emma. You believe in the Easter Bunny. You're soft…and there's nothing wrong with that. I love you just the way you are. You tell me how you want him to die and I'll take care of it for you. It should be *my* hand that ends his life. I won't have a problem sleeping at night. You might. I'm your mate. Let me take this burden."

She seemed to consider it. "I've spent most of my life having nightmares about him. He was my boogeyman, Red. My childhood was happy, and I had a wonderful mom until that night he betrayed my grandpa and went after the VampLycans. He murdered the humans living with us. They were our friends, who had no idea we weren't just like them. It was kind of a hippie community. They all had gardens in their backyards and everyone was very kind. They didn't deserve to be hunted and killed." She paused. "I appreciate you offering but this is something I need to do. I'll be fine with it. If for some reason I chicken out, you can kill him for me. I don't see that happening though. I've wanted that asshole dead since I realized my mom was never coming back."

He nodded. "I'll be with you. Always. You falter, I'll do it."

"Thank you."

He heard someone yell out his name. Emma did as well, and she turned her head in the direction of her room.

"Get dressed." He released her and left the closet, walked through her bedroom, and opened the door to the hallway.

Graves stood near the stairwell. "There you are. This place is more like a hotel than a house. I had no idea what room to go to. Velder wants you."

"How is Malachi?"

"Clean, smells a hell of a lot better, and looks normal." He grinned. "For a Vampire. I have to say, he's larger than most of the ones I've met. I like him. Good sense of humor."

"We'll be right down."

"Hurry up. Velder is in a mood. One of the Vampires tried to run."

"Are they still alive?"

"Yeah. Pest didn't blender his ass, but he did shell and crush his hand." Graves grinned. "I want to see that blender move. Fingers crossed. It sounds gross as hell but I'm lacking any sympathy for those bloodsuckers who started this shit-storm."

Red returned to the closet. Emma had dressed and put on a pair of slip-on canvas shoes. He held out his hand. "It's time."

"I hope we have time to pack." She glanced at her clothes. "I'd like to take them to Alaska with me. I didn't exactly have much in my go bag."

"We'll take the time."

"Will Velder be annoyed with me bringing suitcases?"

"No. There's room on the jet."

He grew quiet, and so did Emma as they took the main stairs down. The Vampires were still in a circle in the living room. The Lycans,

GarLycans, and his clan members surrounded them. Eduardo had inched closer to Paula, hissing words at her. Red cocked his head, listening. The bastard was pleading with her to save his life. Red studied her face, seeing a granite expression without emotion. He doubted the assassin could do anything, regardless of what she wanted. Eduardo would die.

"Grandpa!" Emma tore out of his hold and ran to the tall blond who walked out of the office with his Uncle Velder at his side.

Red watched as the man opened his arms wide, scooped his mate up, and hugged her tight. He tensed, his fingertips tingling, his claws wanting to rip through his skin when the Vampire buried his face in the crook of her neck. He couldn't stop the growl that rumbled from him. He'd kill him if he bit her.

But Malachi lifted his head fast, no blood on his lips, and their gazes locked.

Red tried to calm his anger. The Vampire was Emma's grandfather. Not the enemy. He just didn't like her being held that tight by anyone who wasn't him.

Malachi's eyes narrowed, his nostrils flared, and he glanced down at Emma. The Vampire looked at him again...and his lips compressed into a tight line.

Emma fought tears. She hated crying, but it had been a tough day. "You're okay."

Grandpa hugged her tight again and eased her to her feet. He cupped her chin, studying her face. "You got banged up. What part of calling you 'princess' left you confused? I trained you better, Em."

That helped dry her eyes. Anger sparked as she grasped his hand and removed it from her jaw. "Don't even lecture me, Grandpa. Did you think I *wouldn't* come? Give me a break."

He smiled. "I thought you'd send the VampLycans. Not put your ass right in the line of fire." He glanced up at Velder. "Thank you. I had faith that someone from the clan would show up. I'm sorry for getting you involved but they kept me poisoned and drugged. They also said the entire council was looking for my granddaughter. At some point, she might have left your territory and been captured."

Emma frowned. "How did you get Linda to call the VampLycans?"

Grandpa chuckled, looking down at her. "I embedded a few easily controlled humans with orders to call Howl, Alaska, and say I was searching for you, if I ever called them by phone. Linda was the only human I was able to reach. She hadn't retired from her job yet. Those idiots from the council wanted you. I knew if I left that message on our machine, you'd tell the VampLycans I was in trouble, and they'd come." His expression grew serious. "These morons believed I'd made a deal with them to lure you home. They swore you wouldn't be hurt if I brought you in." He snorted, shooting a glare in their direction. "As if I'd allow you assholes to turn my Emma over to those thugs you call a council." He looked back at Emma. "You were supposed to stay with their clan and keep safe."

Emma wouldn't apologize. "You would have come for *me*."

"I taught you to save yourself, Emma." He glanced at Velder. "Do you have grandchildren yet? They love to frustrate you and drive you insane. They forget that older is wiser."

Velder chuckled. "Just sons. No grandbabies yet. I can't wait."

Her grandpa reached up, tugging on her wet hair. "Who's the one glaring at me?"

Emma backed away and held out her hand to Red. "Grandpa, I'd like you to meet Redson Redwolf."

Red came forward, took her hand, but looked tense. "Sir."

Her grandfather glanced around, and then frowned at Red. "You look just like your father. Klackan didn't come with you?"

Emma opened her mouth but Red spoke first.

"He died, sir."

Her grandpa's grief showed. He reached out to Red, placing a hand on his shoulder. "Your father has always held a special place in my heart. I am deeply wounded to hear this news. You have my sincerest condolences." He briefly glanced down at their joined hands. "Is Emma your mate?"

Red didn't hesitate. "Yes."

Grandpa released his shoulder. "Why haven't you completed the bond?"

"We wanted to get your permission first, sir."

Emma glanced back and forth between the men she loved. Red and her grandpa seemed to have some kind of grim staring contest. Her grandpa finally broke it by glancing at Velder. "Is it allowed? Her father was human, and there's no hiding that. I'm not certain of the laws you may have written."

Velder stepped closer. "It is. My sons mated partial humans. My mate believes it's a family trait our younger generation share." He grinned.

Grandpa cleared his throat. "Emma, may we speak alone?"

She didn't budge. "No."

Grandpa scowled and narrowed his eyes.

"No," she repeated. "You always said you wanted me to be with someone I love, trust, and who makes me happy. That's Red. I want your blessing."

"You have it."

She blew out the breath she'd been holding.

"I just wanted to make sure you're aware of VampLycan culture." He glanced around. "No offense. She's been raised as human as possible. I wanted her to have a normal life."

It was her turn to snort. She focused, clearing her mind, and pushed her thoughts toward her grandpa. *"Don't piss off the people who just saved you, old man. I love Red, and he's worried that you'll attack him. Please smile and be cool with this. I really do love him."*

Her grandpa cocked his head, staring into her eyes. *"I said you have my permission."*

"You look like someone just died. You're not losing me. You're gaining a kick-ass grandson-in-law. And we're both alive. The VampLycans and Red are responsible. Smile, damn it. Act happy."

Grandpa nodded and smiled. *"Better?"*

Emma rolled her eyes. *"You can be such an ass. Tell Red welcome to the family or something."*

"What in the hell is going on?" Velder, asked.

"We're having a private chat," Emma admitted. "Grandpa needed a mental kick in the pants."

Grandpa's smile widened. "Welcome to the family, Red. I'm thrilled that you and my grandbaby are mates." He faced Velder. "Emma was four when she came into my care. She has a unique ability to receive my thoughts and send her own. Her mother could sense her moods in the womb and sometimes catch what she was thinking as a child."

"I didn't know that." Emma was surprised.

"It's only shown itself with family. Your mother, then me." Grandpa shrugged. "It might have been a rare human trait your father had, or maybe some fluke thing that happens with VampLycan and human children. It wasn't as if there were any others like you around to ask."

"What's the distance?"

"Not far." Grandpa answered Velder. "Inside the house, to the front yard. It takes concentration for both of us. We worked on it after I heard some of her stronger thoughts about me." He chuckled. "'He's so mean' were the first words of hers that I heard inside my head. I had yelled at her after she'd jumped out of a tree. She'd seen me do it but didn't understand that she could have broken her legs or worse from such a height, if I hadn't caught her. It took a while for her to learn she can't do what I can. I had to keep reminding her how fragile she is and to accept her limitations."

"Here we go." Emma shook her head.

Grandpa frowned. "What?"

"You've made her feel inferior." Anger tinged Red's tone. "She's *not*. Just different. The sun can't hurt Emma. You'd fry, Malachi."

"I apologize." Grandpa appeared horrified. "That's not how I meant for you to feel."

"Let's deal with family issues later." Velder jerked his head toward the living room and waiting Vampires. "I'm going to talk to Paula, we'll take care of Eduardo, and then we're out of here."

"What are you going to do with the Vampires from the council?" Emma asked.

"I'm going to make a call to their council, tell them where they can pick up their assassins alive, and warn them to stay the fuck away from my clan members." He pointed at Malachi. "You included. How do you feel about returning to Alaska? You're clan. I'm certain you'll want to stay close to Emma."

Emma watched his face for a reaction but he was too good at hiding them. His voice, when he spoke, didn't even give a hint. "Blood would become an issue."

Velder shook his head. "Sometimes VampLycans are born more Vampire. *They* get fed. It's not a problem. The younger ones take a vein from a family member. The older ones get it in bags. The clan is happy to help each other."

Emma stepped closer. "At least come for a while, until things blow over, Grandpa. You know you'd worry about me otherwise." She jerked her thumb toward the Vampires. "Give them a cooling-off period."

He addressed Velder. "I'd be honored."

"Great." Velder paused. "I gave Emma my word she could kill Eduardo. Are you okay with that? He was a member of your nest."

Rage reddened Grandpa's face. "I'll kill that little prick myself."

Emma hadn't considered that he might want to take out Eduardo. She could feel Red tense beside her. "The kill is yours, Grandpa. He murdered my mom but she was also your daughter. Plus, you've spent all this time having to deal with him since he invaded the house." She couldn't imagine what it had been like for her grandpa to be stuffed into his own safe. "Vengeance is yours."

Grandpa reached out and squeezed her shoulder. "Thank you. You don't have to watch. I plan to make him suffer first." He glanced at Red. "Perhaps you should take her somewhere else."

She wanted to groan in frustration, knowing Red would do it.

He surprised her though.

"Emma is strong, and she deserves to witness her mother's murderer being put to death. I'll stand with her."

Hot tears filled her eyes and she blinked them back, smiling up at him.

Red didn't look happy, but he squeezed her hand. "I know how much this matters to you."

"It does."

"Let's get this over with. The sun will go down in a few hours and we have a jet to catch." Velder leaned closer to Malachi. "How do you feel about being flown by a GarLycan? It would save time once we set down in Alaska, to get you under cover before the sun rises."

Grandpa chuckled. "I love new experiences."

"He's an adrenaline junkie," Emma shared with everyone. "You might be sorry you offered. He'll hound Glacier to take him flying if he loves it."

"Shush, Grandchild. Don't spoil my fun."

Emma rolled her eyes. "Don't take hours to kill Eduardo but make it painful, please. I need to pack before we go. I'm not leaving my clothes behind."

They walked in a group toward the Vampires. Eduardo tried to hide behind the Vampires nearest him, as if anyone would forget he was there. Grandpa waded through their bodies, grabbed him by his hair, and dragged him toward the fireplace. None of the council Vamps protested or said a word. They probably feared they'd be next.

"Mal," Eduardo whimpered. "I'm your child!"

Malachi slammed him against the stone, released his hair, and a chill ran down Emma's spine as her grandpa released control of his rage in a wave of menace and Vampire power. Once glance and she was certain everyone else felt it too. A few VampLycans lifted their eyebrows but didn't step back. The Vamps on the floor trembled.

Red pulled her close, putting his arm around her. She curled into his side but didn't look away.

"You killed my child. I ordered you not to go after Kallie and the others. They were under our protection. You betrayed me, went to another nest, and took my baby from me."

Emma lowered her gaze when the bleeding started. Her grandpa had always been kind, sweet, and gentle with her. Unless they were training. The way he used his claws to rip open parts of Eduardo made her feel ill. Red didn't try to pull her away though. He held her tight, staying at her side.

Eduardo's shrieks and pleas for mercy didn't end his suffering.

"I sentence you to the death I once saved you from!" her grandfather thundered.

Emma lifted her gaze as Velder offered a sword to Malachi. He used it, severing Eduardo's head. It hit the floor, rolled, and both parts of him ashed.

It was done. The man from her nightmares would never get the chance to hurt or hunt her again.

Grandpa found her gaze, holding it.

She knew him well. He was worried that she'd see him differently. "I love you."

Her grandfather placed the sword on the mantel.

Red eased his hold on her. "Let's pack your things. We don't need to see my uncle threaten these bastards again."

She agreed. Her gaze when to her grandpa.

He must have heard them from across the room. "Go. I'll be up in a few minutes to pack my stuff. We're never coming back here. I'm going to burn it to the ground."

There must be a lot of blood in the house for such an extreme measure. Who knew what the Vampires had done while they'd been there? For all she knew, there were bodies hidden. It was a grim thought. The evidence would need to be destroyed.

* * * * *

Velder watched Red and Emma disappear upstairs and motioned Malachi to walk with him. The Vampire followed him to a corner of the room.

"Thank you for coming."

Velder smiled. "You knew we would."

"I hoped. You VampLycans are honorable and treat your friends well."

"We learned from you." Velder had missed his old friend. "Are you truly accepting of Red and Emma being mates?"

"Yes. As long as she's accepted in the clan."

"You both are considered clan. You're the one who left *us*. You weren't asked to go."

"I had no choice."

Velder remembered. "What happened to your children with Vampire traits?"

Sadness filled Malachi's eyes. "They didn't like my rules or the way I kept trying to convince them that humans mattered. Youth are often headstrong and arrogant. They fled the city together one night. I've not seen them since."

"I'm sorry, my old friend." Velder couldn't imagine his children disappearing from his life.

"It was for the best."

"I don't know how you can say that."

Malachi's expression hardened, his eyes going cold. "I probably would have had to ash them in time. No father should have to kill his own children. They showed little empathy or compassion toward their mother and sister." He lowered his voice. "I felt relief when they left. They hunted at night without me because I didn't feel safe leaving my beloved mate and daughter unprotected against my own children."

Velder reached out and gripped Malachi's shoulders, giving them a firm squeeze. "I'm sorry."

"I am as well."

"I'm glad you're returning to Alaska."

Malachi smiled but sadness returned to his eyes. "I just wish my beloved were still alive."

Velder gave him another squeeze and released him. "I can't imagine losing my mate. I'm sorry, friend."

"I have Emma. That's more family than most other Vampires have."

"You have us as well, Malachi."

Chapter Fifteen

Red carried in both of her suitcases and then went back out on the porch of his cabin to grab their travel bags. Emma waved goodbye to Lake, who'd driven them to the cabin in his off-road vehicle from where the small planes had dropped them off outside of Howl. She was glad to be back in Alaska.

Red and her went inside and he locked the door. "Do you want to go see Malachi?"

"The sun is up. He needs uninterrupted day sleep after being hurt." She didn't want to think about what her grandpa had been through. "He agreed to stay here for a few months. We'll have plenty of time to talk."

"I'm glad he took us becoming mates so well."

"I told you so." She reached up and placed her hands on his chest. "He's not an evil Vampire."

"He wasn't thrilled."

"We talked a little on the jet while you were using the bathroom. He was just worried about me adjusting to living with VampLycans."

Red snorted. "Says the Vampire."

She laughed. "I pointed that out and told him the hardest part to adjust to was how tan all of you are."

Red smiled. "What was he worried about? Everyone in the clan accepts you."

"He missed Jarred shifting in the living room. Grandpa wasn't sure if I'd seen you on four legs. I told him I had. He asked if I was afraid and I told him no, because it was still you. You'd never hurt me."

"That's it?"

"Yes. He's actually relieved we're mates. He said you'll treat me better than a human. Of course, then he pointed out he couldn't control your mind to remember anniversaries and birthdays. I told him to use his mouth and remind you that way."

"You and your grandfather have a twisted sense of humor."

"I know, and now we're yours. What does that say about *you*?"

"That I really love you. Are you hungry? Tired?"

"I slept on your lap during the flight and ate on the plane. I'm good. Are we returning to the den?"

"There's no reason to. Uncle Velder set the assassins straight, they're afraid to come near us or the GarLycans. I took you there to keep you safe. No one is coming after you here."

She thought about Velder letting the Vampires go before the house was set on fire. She grinned. "That was *so* funny when Glacier and Tempest were diving from the sky at them while they ran for their lives."

He chuckled. "I loved it when Pest grabbed the slowest one and flew him by his foot over the rest of them, then dropped him on the one in the lead."

She cracked up. That *had* been amusing. "I would never dare shorten his name like that to his face."

"Me either. Glacier is his brother though."

She smiled up at him. "Mate me, Red."

He didn't hesitate to scoop her into his arms and carry her up the stairs.

She wrapped her arms around his neck. "No argument there, huh?"

"Fuck no. I've waited long enough." He didn't stop until they reached his bedroom. He kicked the door closed behind them and gently put her on the bed. "Get naked."

She slipped off her shoes, reaching for her shirt next. Red just tore at his clothes, tossing them toward the nearest wall.

"What do I need to do?"

"It will come naturally. Trust your instincts."

She nodded, sliding off the bed to be rid of her leggings. Red finished undressing first and tore off the covers from the bed, down to the sheets.

She turned, meeting his gaze. "For a while, I never thought we'd be alone."

He came around the bed and lifted her off her feet, kissing her. She moaned against his mouth and wrapped her legs around his waist. He hoisted her higher and climbed on the bed, gently pinning her under him. She loved the feel of his hot skin pressed against hers. His hands roamed her body, making her burn with need.

He smelled amazing, and she remembered that pheromone thing, wondering if he'd send her into heat again. She embraced it all. This was a part of her life she looked forward to with Red as her mate.

He tore his mouth from hers and began to trail kisses along her throat, sliding down her body. She grabbed his hair, pulling him back up. "I'm so wet. Get in me. I don't need foreplay."

His eyes were golden with that amazing glow to them. She didn't look away.

"I want to taste you. You smell so fucking good."

Her nipples beaded. "That's so sexy when you growl at me."

"It's sexy as fuck when your thighs are wrapped around me."

"In me, Red. Now."

"So fucking demanding." He dipped his head, latching on to the tip of her breast, and gave it a nip. She jolted under him. It was almost painful, but it felt too good. "Patience, Emma."

"Fuck that. I've wanted you since the night before last, when I had to sleep next to you in that bed and we couldn't do more than cuddle. There was no privacy on the jet except the bathroom and I didn't want to piss anyone off by locking us in there for a while, since there was only one."

Red lifted up, holding her gaze. "You don't have fangs. I'll slice open my skin when the time comes. Drink from me when I bite you."

She felt a moment of uncertainty but then gazed into his eyes, nodding. "Got it."

He reached between them, teasing her clit with his finger. She moaned and adjusted her legs around his waist, using his body to wiggle her hips to urge him on.

"Fuck, you're so ready."

"Told you."

He stopped playing with her, grabbed himself, and adjusted until the head of his cock pressed against her. He rubbed the crown through her slit, teasing. She dug her fingernails into his skin, not being careful with them.

"Now," she demanded. "Please, Red. I ache for you."

He pressed against her opening, released his shaft, and braced his arms as he thrust forward, entering her deep and fast.

Emma threw her head back and cried out his name. Red snarled then began to move fast and hard. Pleasure built quickly and Emma knew she wouldn't last long before she came. She was thrilled Red wasn't human; sex with him felt a thousand times better than anything she'd experienced with her exes.

He buried his face in her throat, ran his tongue across her skin, then twisted his arm on the other side. Looked down, Emma watched his claws slide out of the tips of his fingers. He dragged one sharp tip along the skin just under his shoulder. Blood flowed—and she felt his fangs against her neck.

She wanted to bite him as he fucked her harder, faster. She lifted her head, locking her mouth over the small cut, and his blood hit her tongue. Emma opened her mouth wider and bit around it, sucking and swallowing. Red bit her back, snarling.

That was it. The world exploded inside her mind from how hard she came.

Emma stopped swallowing when his wound started to close, and then Red removed his fangs from her throat. He licked at the bite. Both of them panted hard, and she smiled.

"Wow. I think I saw stars."

"*I'd give you ever damn one of them, baby.*"

"That's so sweet."

"What is?" Red looked at her. His eyes were utterly black now, and his voice came out super deep.

She frowned. "That was weird."

"What? You don't like the taste of my blood?"

"No. How drastically you changed your voice."

"What are you talking about?" He frowned back. "*Did I take too much blood? Damn it. I should have been more careful.*"

"I like it rough."

His eyes widened, and he lifted his head more, peering at her. "Look at my mouth."

She lowered her gaze. "I love your lips. I want to nibble on them."

"*I love you more than life.*"

His mouth didn't move…but she heard him. She was stunned as she locked her gaze to his.

"*You hear me, don't you, baby?*"

She nodded and concentrated. "*Can you hear me?*"

He grinned. "I can. We're tightly linked. This shouldn't have happened so fast. It usually isn't possible with humans, but you must have a lot of VampLycan blood. I hear you really clearly. Talk to me again."

"*I love you too. Why do you look freaked out just a tiny bit?*"

"Amazing," he breathed. "And I'm not freaked out. Just surprised. You're so clear!" He reached between them and pinched her nipple.

She jumped. "Ouch!"

He frowned. "I didn't feel that."

"*I* did! What the hell?"

"Tightly bonded VampLycan mates can feel what the other does during sex. It's a physical connection."

That sounded fun, and she was slightly disappointed to not experience it. "Maybe it will happen with time."

"Maybe. But it doesn't matter. I have no complaints. I can hear you in my head." He grinned. *"I fucking love you."*

"I'm all yours."

"I just hope I can't hear your grandfather." He slid from her body. "Well, *that* softened my dick. Let's make a rule we never talk about him while in bed."

She laughed as he rolled over, and followed him, curling up against his side. "Deal."

"My mate."

She grinned, putting her head on his chest, listening to his heartbeat. "My mate."

He suddenly laughed.

"What's so funny?"

"It just hit me that this is real, and I didn't have to kill a Vampire to keep you. Thank you, Emma."

"Does this mean you won't be so grumpy? I kind of thought it was cute."

He rolled again, pinning her under him once more. "You want grumpy?"

"I want everything you've got to give me, Red."

"You're going to make me hide eggs and shit when we have kids, aren't you?"

She was confused.

"That damn Easter Bunny."

"You're thinking about that *now*?"

"That would make me grumpy." He leaned in and brushed a kiss on her lips and grinned. "But I'd do it. You want kids, don't you?"

"I'm forty. I'm ready to have mini-Redson babies whenever you are. How old are you?"

He just grinned.

"Come on, tell me."

"Older than you."

"You're such an ass."

"I'm *your* ass." He slid his hand down her side and under her butt, giving her a squeeze. "And this is *my* ass. It's better than grabbing your chin, right?"

She laughed. "Much."

His expression grew pensive.

"What are you thinking about?"

His eyes lightened to their normal shade, the black receding. "I'm just imagining our future. Having kids. Watching cartoons about human holidays that I'm certain you'll insist on. Probably even lugging in a dead tree you'll want to decorate." His lips twitched, and his eyes lightened further, turning golden. "I'm looking forward to all of it with you."

She blinked back tears. "You're the best thing that's ever happened to me, Red."

"Right back at you. Let's strengthen our bond more." He let go of her ass and reached up, brushing his thumb over her one of the bruises on her arm from her fight with the Vampires, already fading. "You're healing faster. I hated seeing bruises on you."

"Forget about that." She slid her fingers into his hair. "Make love to me."

"Happily, for the rest of our lives."

About the Author

NY Times and USA Today Bestselling Author

I'm a full-time wife, mother, and author. I've been lucky enough to have spent over two decades with the love of my life and look forward to many, many more years with Mr. Laurann. I'm addicted to iced coffee, the occasional candy bar (or two), and trying to get at least five hours of sleep at night.

I love to write all kinds of stories. I think the best part about writing is the fact that real life is always uncertain, always tossing things at us that we have no control over, but when writing you can make sure there's always a happy ending. I love that about being an author. My favorite part is when I sit down at my computer desk, put on my headphones to listen to loud music to block out everything around me, so I can create worlds in front of me.

For the most up to date information, please visit my website. www.LaurannDohner.com

CPSIA information can be obtained
at www.ICGtesting.com
Printed in the USA
BVHW03s1836140818
524497BV00001B/98/P